Finding

the

Holy Path

HERTFORDSHIRE PRESS

Published in United Kingdom
Hertfordshire Press © 2014
(Imprint of Silk Road Media)

Suite 125, 43 Bedford Street
Covent Garden, London
WC2 9HA United Kingdom
www.hertfordshirepress.com

Finding the Holy Path by Shahsanem Murray

Typeset by Aleksandra Vlasova
Translated by Matthew Naumann
Edited by Laura Hamilton

British Library Catalogue in Publication Data
A catalogue record for this book is available from the British Library
Library of Congress in Publication Data
A catalogue record for this book has been requested

ISBN 978-0-9927873-9-4

Contents

Acknowledgments

I would like to express heartfelt thanks firstly to my grandfather Toktogul who passed down all of these wonderful tales to me; my family, colleagues and friends for their continuous support, my father, Sartov Abakir; my main adviser and proof reader, Gordon Murray; Russian editor A. Sydykbaev; translator Matthew Naumann, editor Laura Hamilton, and the "OCA" group's publisher Marat Akhmedjanov, designer Alexandra Vlasova, and illustrator Varvara Perekrest.

It was a great team and many of my wonderful friends, who provided much of the inspiration for this book, may even have become models for some of the characters…

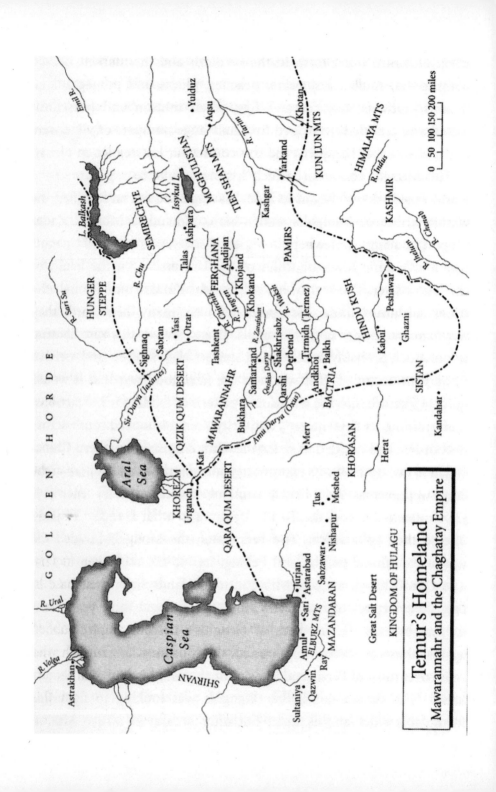

Temur's Homeland
Mawarannahr and the Chaghatay Empire

SHAHSANEM MURRAY

Finding

the

Holy Path

London 2014

Prologue

History is all around us and as it mysteriously sails through time past you and me, there are occasions when it causes us to stop for a moment and simply reflect...

And when we allow our minds to draw parallels between the world that you and I share in the present, and the mysteries of past eras, opportunities can arise for doorways to open to a greater understanding of the lives of those who have left a mark on our common history.

This book seeks to transport you back in time to events that occurred along the Great Silk Road around the middle of the sixteenth century.

These stories have been orally passed down from generation to generation and thus preserved, can now be enjoyed today.

Working on this book, I made many intriguing discoveries since history is full of illusions and secret agendas.

I am presenting you with a fictitious interpretation of the origins of just some of the events described in these fantastic stories and in tandem with historical facts; hope to be able to offer an insight into those characters who had such a huge impact on world heritage.

The passionate love story of the Northern Kyrgyz Khan, Tagay-Bii and Tomchi, the Bukharain beauty, takes us to a magical land called Fergana, and the pre-destined course of their relationship touches the soul particularly deeply. We also follow the story of their son, Kara-Choro, whose innate fortitude and strength of character equipped him well to endure and survive all of the challenges which fate had in store for him.

The book seamlessly reveals the invisible web that links the destinies of all the many characters, taking the reader from Scotland's capital city Edinburgh, both past and present, into the vast territory of ancient Russia.

A key aspect is the great Library, which the first Russian Tsar, Ivan the Terrible, founded during his lifetime.

Academics from the Tatar nobility played important roles in the foundation of the Library after the weakening and eventual collapse of the Golden Horde, which resulted in them being transferred into the service of Muscovy (Moscow). Here, we are introduced to the Tatar nobleman-scholar Eshen-Kareg and his three sons: Ibrahim, Sadyk and Yusuf who worked under the constant threat of execution and torture by the Russian Tsar. The sons' subsequent escape and their new lives played a key role in the creation of new clans along the Great Silk Road.

Through such mystical traces and echoes of the past, we are invited to step back in time and for a moment, immerse ourselves in a unique period of Central Asian antiquity.

Shahsanem Murray
Author

Chapter I

Echoes of the Past in the Present

The strong storm that raged all night caused Edinburgh's residents no end of trouble. A piercing wind swept across the city's rooftops and the tall clay chimneys emitted dark blue, harsh-smelling smoke which in turn enveloped the city as if eager to catch it in a crushing embrace.

People covered their faces, hiding from the acrid smoke that remorselessly covered the city's stone walls with black soot.

Outbreaks of fire were frequent, and from time to time, the townsfolk were forced to quickly rescue all that was dear to them, including their own lives. City officials introduced legislation to ban thatched roofs, in an effort to prevent burning straw being spread by the strong winds that were so common.

Few people wondered why roofs were often accidentally set alight on mornings when there was little breeze...

Reforms were passed and Edinburgh gradually became the administrative centre of Scotland...

***

... A grey and leaden sky overshadowed the strange morning sunrise, and only occasionally did bright rays of sun and fragments of blue manage to break through the clouds. A small dark cloud floated slowly past one of Edinburgh's tenements on the fifth floor of which the owner of a small bookshop busily marched along the corridor and up and down the wooden stairs to the basement, each time carrying several books and manuscripts.

On the stone floor of the basement, onto which a strong cold wind chased through all apertures, the shop owner hurriedly filled a voluminous bag, casting aside anything deemed unnecessary and carefully packing only the essentials.

The old man was seventy years old, grey-haired and stooped, and attired in a dark tartan jacket. He was known as Miller, and served as a clerk to Adam Smith, the famous economist.

The jacket that Miller never removed protected him from the building's damp. Sometimes he even slept in his clothes to keep himself warm in the poorly heated little room where he spent his days, painstakingly transcribing academic theses.

Adam Smith's popularity grew. He sought to surround himself with intelligent and open-minded people during a period when a great number opposed his activities.

This was also a matter of concern for his personal clerk, old Miller, who the day before the events described herein, had transferred Smith's most valuable works to a secret labyrinth outside the city.

The heavy wooden door suddenly creaked open and in the dark corridor leading to the basement appeared the monstrous silhouette of a large man in a black cloak and maroon coloured mask.

The owner of the quarters instinctively recoiled to the opposite wall but immediately realized that it was too late to flee and there was nowhere to hide.

"Stand still," ordered the man in a sharp, commanding voice. His face was completely hidden by the mask, apart from a slit which revealed fierce, bloodshot eyes.

"I'm sorry, but who are you?" asked Miller in a trembling, geriatric voice.

"Who am I?!... Let me tell you: I'm the chief of the Blackdales clan!" An evil laugh erupted from the man in black.

"Oh, dear God! So the rumours are true?! I should have heeded the warnings and begun my preparations much earlier," groaned Miller. His bare legs gave way and he collapsed helplessly onto the bag which he was in the process of packing. On the wall next to him, a silver lamp was quietly burning, filling the entire basement with the pungent smell of scorched wick-wool.

"Rumours? Preparations? What are you talking about old man? I've no interest in any of that or even in you! Just tell me where I can find Adam Smith!"

"Excuse me, who are you talking about? I do not know this name, sir. And anyway, at my age, with my senility…" Miller the clerk tried to laugh it off.

"How dare you jest with me? Where is he?" shouted the man. Now enraged, he ran at poor Miller and, ignoring the old man's rasping pleas, grabbed him by the throat and dragged him along the wooden corridor and up the staircase to the top flat.

"I beg you, don't do anything stupid! I don't know who you are talking about!" begged Miller in a husky voice.

"You imbecile! You know perfectly well!" With one kick, the tall man smashed the window in the fifth floor room and swung Miller's upturned and decrepit body through it, hissing furiously. "Right! I'm asking you for the last time: where is Adam Smith?"

"Have mercy on me, sir! I am the keeper of many mysteries hidden deep in the centuries!" Despite a suspicion that there would be no leniency, old Miller continued to beg.

"The only mystery that interests me at this moment is the location of your master, you idiot!" The man in the black cloak laughed viciously as he held tightly to old Miller's bare feet.

"Alright, alright, I'll tell you! I beg you, excuse me my senile forgetfulness! I've only just remembered who we're talking about!" cried Miller, seeking mercy.

"Well, about time!" crowed the tall man as he pulled old Miller from the open window and back into the room.

Miller lay on the floor for several minutes trying to catch his breath, whilst absently staring at the masked stranger, who called himself the Head of the Blackdales clan.

"Well, get on with it! Start drawing me a map of his location!" The Blackdales chief, growing impatient with the old man, picked up a blank sheet of paper from the floor and threw it at his face.

"Just a minute! Just a minute!" Pale with fear, Miller began to grope around for the silver lamp, which also served as an inkwell. Then, recalling that the lamp was still in the basement, he turned to his tormentor and whimpered in terror.

"What? What is it now?" The villain bent over Miller, intending to cuff him across the head. At that moment they suddenly heard the whistling sound of a swinging metal blade before it plunged into the body of the man in the black cloak. The chief jerked as blood spewed from his mouth. Slowly swaying, he averted his astonished gaze away from the dumbfounded clerk towards his attacker, but as he lurched forwards, his legs buckled beneath him and he tumbled through the open window. All that was heard was the dull thud of his heavy body as it landed on the street, breaking every bone as it fell.

Miller, in a state of shock, remained slumped on the floor as he gazed in amazement at his saviour.

"What, are you still here, my dear man, and all alone?" He stared at the clerk. "You were warned, weren't you? There's not a minute to lose! Pack your things. We've been waiting for you at the labyrinth outside the city for some time!"

Standing in front of Miller was middle -aged man with light brown eyes, dressed in a blue coat and armed with a long, ancient dagger from which the Blackdales leader's blood still dripped. A barely noticeable, gentle mocking could be discerned in his soothing voice. Holding out his free hand, he helped Miller sit up and passed him his shoes.

"Who are you?" Miller asked the stranger in a trembling voice, as his stiff fingers fought to tie up his laces.

"I am one of the Peterson Clan, the White Knights, who protect the interests of innocent people!" The stranger introduced himself in a rather derisive yet proud tone and then guided the still traumatized clerk down the stairs.

"We must gather up my things from the basement and also collect another item which I need for my work," Adam Smith's scribe gradually began to regain his senses as he and the Clan Peterson White Knight walked down the old wooden staircase to the basement. Once there, they amassed everything that Miller needed. When momentarily out of sight of his protector, Miller seized the chance to stealthily pick up the now extinguished silver lamp from the stone floor and without emptying its contents, tucked it into his shirt. Together, they exited onto the street where two bridled horses were tethered to a tree. As they walked, the scribe involuntarily stole a glance at the place beneath the broken window where lay the Blackdales chief's shattered body.

"Have mercy on his sinful soul, O Lord!" Miller raised his eyes to the grey, leaden sky.

"Hurry up, there are many more of them in the city," Peterson's voice was soft but authoritative as he helped Miller onto his horse.

"Evil alas, does not disappear with the death of just one man" whispered Miller. The pair glanced repeatedly behind and all around them as they rode along the city's stone bridge towards the North Sea...

***

The alarm clock rang twice and Miss J.M woke up in a sweat, panting anxiously.

"Oh! What a dream!" Pressing her palm to her forehead and wiping her damp neck with a soft towel, she slipped her feet into the warm slippers she had brought from home, threw on a luxurious white dressing gown and walked slowly to the kitchen. Switching on the television to hear the morning news, she unhurriedly made herself a strong coffee.

Afterwards, with the window ajar to let in the fresh November air, she spent a little time studying documents on her laptop whilst making notes. Then, satisfied with what she had achieved, she quickly got ready for work.

The radical Blackdales group most likely existed as the subject of mystical legends. Documents report that the ruthless and bloodthirsty Blackdales planned criminal acts against Adam Smith and that some of his scientific work was rescued by the Peterson white knights who nevertheless, failed to prevent arson and the subsequent destruction of the church premises.

Chapter II

Objects from a Bygone Age

A light, drizzling rain that had lasted for three days, coupled with the coolness of the autumn air, invigorated all of those participating in that day's seminar at the Legends and Myths Revisited Centre (LMR), helping them to focus on the sublime and abstract concepts being presented by the speakers.

The haar that shrouded Edinburgh gave the Centre, a Gothic church near a city park on Lauriston Road, a mysterious and ghostly appearance that reflected the theme of the lecture given by Dr Brandon Silver, LMR's founder and executive director.

The doctor was powerfully built and slightly short in stature, with a clean shaven head and large horn-rimmed glasses. At the podium facing an audience of twenty-five to thirty, he stood with his legs apart and head bent forward, as if ready to physically challenge anyone who questioned the validity of his thesis. Speaking with deep conviction he began:

"Now let's consider this fire which I've just described, a phenomenal event which could even be perceived as mystical; a fire which destroyed the vast majority of artefacts which had been stored for centuries in the vaults of this church. Our collection was invaluable to world science and culture in all respects. Indeed, it is testimony to its high regard that our generous patrons stepped forward to provide the funding for the rebuild: painstaking work that has taken an entire decade of invaluable effort and labour."

The Doctor nodded in the direction of a group of individuals who were standing somewhat apart and who were not slow to ceremoniously bow in return.

"Work by the Archivists and findings from our own research have shown that the material was originally divided into thematic categories, spanning an expanse of geographical regions and historical periods. Items from all sections were discovered almost fully or partially destroyed by the fire, with the exception of one group: that which related to the period of the 'Great Silk Road.' A realm and here I am not afraid to use grand language that uniquely embodied whole worlds and eras. In contrast to the others, artefacts in this category appeared to have been so completely engulfed by the fire that there remained absolutely no evidence of their existence: not a single shard or even any ashes. In other words, this group of exhibits simply disappeared without trace!"

The doctor walked over to the table to the left of the podium on which stood a laptop and a decanter of mineral water. He took a sip of water from a tumbler and then bending over the computer, and using his index finger to balance his glasses on the bridge of his nose, asked the audience to open the hand-out at the page containing an illustrated list of the Centre's lost items.

"As you know the Centre suffered a degree of looting after the fire and surviving objects are sometimes discovered in certain antique shops in and around Edinburgh, but none have ever appeared that belong to the Great Silk Road. There can only be one possible conclusion: the artefacts in this category were stolen and the church was set on fire to hide the theft! What is more, the theft was not perpetrated by ordinary criminals for sale on the black market, but by people with a very specific purpose. 'What purpose?' you may ask! Unfortunately, we can only surmise."

Dr Silver's conclusion was met with growing murmurs of amazement from the audience.

J.M, Dr Silver's assistant, was a tall, thirty-five year old Asian woman with smooth opaque skin and long, slender fingers. Her large brown eyes were framed by beautiful long lashes. Dressed in a formal blue jacket and trousers, white blouse and warm white scarf, wrapped around her graceful neck as protection from the cold, she sat in a window alcove to the right of the podium, transcribing the seminar. As she worked, her heart pounded with excitement and as her breasts rose, waves of violet, green and crimson light, falling from the stained glass Gothic pastoral window, washed over her body.

She was excited for two reasons. Firstly, Dr Silver had today announced the results of the Centre's intensive analytical work of the past year, and the conclusions which he just presented to the audience were no longer just guesswork, but well-reasoned and documented facts. The subject of their research had inevitable and major public resonance and threatened to significantly alter the cultural and historical profile of Edinburgh and even create a palpable socio-psychological imbalance amongst its residents. In fact, the near destruction of Archibald Scott's 1859 Gothic church, one of Edinburgh's main historical attractions, had been attributed to one of a series of wildfires which had led to the issue of a whole host of new fire regulations by the city authorities. But was there now proof that this fire had been well planned and methodically executed by some criminal group?

Moreover, had its sole purpose been to hide the trail of theft of some trinkets from the South East of the Eurasian continent? Intriguing to the man on the street, it also seriously affected the credibility of many serious academic researchers, including Dr Silver's colleagues from the University of Edinburgh, on whose recommendation a certain and eager Miss J.M had been appointed assistant to the executive director of the LMR Centre three years ago.

Secondly, and this was the main issue, J.M had a personal motive that twelve years ago, had prompted her to come to Scotland to join the Art and Literature of Ancient Celts Faculty at Edinburgh University. What Dr Brandon Silver had said today inexplicably reminded her of a tape recording of stories narrated long ago by her grandfather, a white-bearded old man named Toktogul. J.M had then been a little girl with pigtails in the village in Central Asia where she often spent her summer holidays. The stories spoke of distant wanderings, eternal love, and the insidious intrigues of enemies. They also referred to items that had magical properties. These were objects of desire, reasons for discord and persecution, pledges of fidelity to one's people and love for a woman. What was perceived at the time to be subject of a wonderful fairy-tale gradually began to point towards something more tangible. And today, J.M. had begun to acknowledge more keenly, that the descriptions of the objects in the stories told by old Toktogul, were almost entirely consistent with Dr Silver's list of artefacts from the category which had disappeared from the burnt down church.

With trepidation and almost childlike impatience she helped the Doctor in his work to restore the lost church collection and the related archival documentation. Together they developed the idea to expand the Centre and give the public greater access to information about the real meaning of the military, political and commercial units in the Eurasian continent, the role of individuals unjustly ignored by historical science, and how philosophies of past centuries shaped modern society. Dr Silver and his colleagues had invested all of their energy in this research, regarding it as a fascinating, and incredible adventure in search of hitherto unknown material that could transform contemporary understanding of world history...

Having collected all the paperwork and switched off the multimedia equipment used during the presentation, J.M. approached the Doctor. Since he was surrounded by members of the audience she had to wait for a moment before she could distract him from the endless questions raining down on him.

"I'm sorry, Doctor, it's time for me to go," she whispered. "I'm meeting Mr Laird at six o'clock at the city notary office to discuss the acquisition of a private collection of archival material from the Edinburgh Port Register."

"Of course, dear Miss J.M, please be on your way!" Dr Silver turned to look at her with flashing blue eyes, which could at once appear triumphantly delighted and detachedly sceptical. On this occasion they expressed a deep gratitude for her professional dedication but sometimes, in rare moments of euphoria, they had been known to reveal the pent-up adoration of a mature man for a beautiful young woman. Now distracted by other matters he turned away, dismissing her with the reminder: "Do not forget that next week we are having a discussion on the Scottish roots of Michel Lermont". He named the Russian poet in the French manner. "Many have expressed an interest in attending the seminar. See you soon, dear Miss J.M!

At the end of the gallery leading to the Centre's exit, J.M. ran into Jane McKendry, the elderly and dour custodian of both the church and the Centre. Mrs McKendry arrived early each morning and left late at night, and it was her job to ensure that the heavy doors were always securely closed.

Despite her tendency to dither, and to the surprise of Dr Silver and J.M, she performed the task flawlessly and methodically. Dr Silver sometimes teased her because of her gloomy disposition, playfully winking at her and inquiring "Well, how are you this morning, our delightful Mrs McKendry?" In response, he received a vague suggestion that he get on with his work, and her pointed glance at his bare head made it clear that she had received attention from academics far more attractive than him.

Unusually, Mrs McKendry was not alone this evening, but on seeing J.M the stranger in a dark cloak who had been standing at her side, turned away and disappeared into the unlit gallery. "A lot of unusual things have happened today" thought J.M. Nodding politely at the custodian, she strained to see what was going on at the back of the Centre. As she headed for the exit, she noticed something odd: there, barely visible in the light of the dying candle which she and the Doctor had lit at the door that very morning, lurked the dark cloaked stranger, barely discernible amongst the stone figurative statues which adorned the inside of the Centre.

A strange and unpleasant sensation swept over her. Pausing in her tracks, she asked herself whether she should know this person: Was it some colleague she couldn't quite recognize? Curious, and rather anxious, she watched as the stranger began to drift towards the altar. Although she couldn't be sure, the broad shoulders and gait implied that the long cloak concealed the figure of a man.

Then, glancing at her watch, her attention returned to her imminent meeting and with that, her unease abated. Putting up her umbrella she crossed the threshold into the world outside the Centre.

As she wandered through the rain-swept Edinburgh evening, key moments of the day and indeed, thoughts about the city she loved, tumbled though her mind.

The city had its own view on things connected with the past. To its inhabitants it displayed a father's indulgence, singing in unison with modern times while proudly upholding the heritage of the streets and buildings and their echoes of bygone days. Whilst studying at the University of Edinburgh, J.M periodically slipped out of the hatch of the attic of the top-floor flat which she shared with other students and took daring walks across the city's rooftops. From this secret vantage point, she delighted in the patterns created by the clusters of chimneys of all shapes and sizes as they stretched towards the horizon. As they puffed away, she liked to imagine what conversations they might have enjoyed about their owners and how well heated their homes were, or about the colliers and their production of "black gold", the salvation of many generations of Edinburgh's residents. Up there, the sunrises were magical as the North Sea appeared to gently caress and rock a great ball of fire as rose slowly from waves awash with pulsating streams of oranges, pinks and reds.

On route to her meeting with Mr. Laird, she found herself lingering in front of an antique shop located in the basement of a small, unimposing tenement building on the Royal Mile, three blocks from the notary's office. "How very strange", thought J.M. She had never noticed this shop before, even though she was well acquainted with all of the agencies and establishments that dealt with antiques in Edinburgh. She still had half an hour to spare before her appointment, so making a snap decision, J.M. pulled the handle of the massive door and stepped inside.

As the door closed heavily behind her, she immediately experienced a sense of being plunged into a different dimension. It felt as if she had entered a massive kaleidoscope, filled with a multitude of objects and images from an equally diverse range of epochs and regions: a place where everything seemed interconnected by some universal predestination.

Overcoming a sudden surge of fervor, she approached the counter where the proprietor was deep in conversation with two other clients but all three fell silent as they turned towards her. The dealer, a swarthy older man with bushy white eyebrows and grey eyes that seemed somehow familiar, smiled pleasantly and looked at her inquisitively. The two visitors also stared at her with interest and they too vaguely reminded her of people from her past.

Miss J.M, however, was so transfixed by the objects arranged on the shelf behind them, that she barely registered their reaction. Later, when recalling her first impression of the shop, she came to the conclusion that the seemingly random array of antiques, which included watches, spears, lockets, vintage clothes, magnifying glasses, miniature cups, globes , precious stone rings and many things besides, had actually been arranged in a carefully, pre-ordained sequence.

It was as though each and every item had been placed according to its significance to the shop's owner but they had also been displayed to capture the imaginations of the customers and to penetrate and make connections with their subconscious memories and aspirations. And J.M was not immune from this as her eyes rested upon one particular object positioned on a shelf above the shopkeeper's head.

After a long silence she addressed the old man: "Good afternoon! Please may I take a closer look at that silver lamp?"

"Just a moment," answered the grey-eyed dealer, politely excusing himself from his two clients who were happy to explore the other treasures hidden deep within the salon.

"Here you are *ma Cherie*, though I beg you to be careful with it," the dealer smiled as he handed her the lamp.

"Do you know where it's from?" she asked, breaking into a spontaneous smile as she took the lamp from him.

"Oh, what I know about the story of this lamp is so complicated that I would have to refer to the files in my archive. However, if you leave me your address, I will copy the documentation for you and at the first opportunity, send it on by post. Alternatively, you could come by tomorrow morning; I'll make some good coffee and together we can search for any information which might be of interest to you." The jovial proposal was delivered with a radiant smile.

"I'm afraid that I can't promise to make it for coffee but I'll leave my address and look forward to hearing from you. Meanwhile, I'll buy the lamp and take it away with me just now. Politely thanking the dealer, J.M then enquired about the price.

"Twenty five pounds, *ma Cherie*," answered the dealer.

The two other clients, who until now had been absorbed by objects displayed on the walls, returned to the counter and delicately waiting their moment, advised her to bargain with the dealer.

She still had a strange feeling that she had seen them somewhere before. Frustratingly, however, she could not remember where, when or in what circumstances. Her attention had been fully absorbed by the lamp. Thinking quickly, she decided to play along with these gentlemen, and they haggled until a price had been reached that suited both she and the dealer. Satisfied, the "support group" then clapped their hands with childlike joy. "I wonder what they're so excited about?" she thought. It was certainly an extraordinary situation, since it was unusual for anyone to haggle in shops such as this. J.M. distractedly patted her long eyelashes.

"It seems like customs from the Oriental bazaar have arrived in Scotland!"

In any case, she hadn't had so much fun shopping for a long time. The antique dealer wrapped up the lamp and as she left her address. J.M. apologized in advance in case she would be unable to come for coffee. They again agreed that if they did not see each other again, he would post her the archived information about the lamp.

Clutching her purchase, J.M. hurried to the notary's office. It was only when she arrived, that she realized that the purchase had been the most impulsive she had made in her entire life, especially since she couldn't pin down why she had been drawn to this little lamp. In addition, she couldn't stop wondering why she felt so sure that she had seen the antique shop owner and his two visitors somewhere before.

As a consequence of her meeting with Mr. Laird, a trade broker contracted by the Centre to conclude the agreement for its latest acquisition of antiques, J.M. found herself laden with a hefty bundle of yellowing tomes containing port of registration journals for commercial navigation in Scotland for the sixteenth to the eighteenth centuries. Burdened by the load, J.M decided to abandon her plan for an extended evening walk through Edinburgh and instead, head for home. On the way she went into a local hardware shop and bought some wool, asking the elderly shopkeeper to demonstrate how to prepare a wick for natural fat. Afterwards, she called in at one of her favorite cafes where she settled herself down in a warm and comfortable corner and ordering a hot chamomile tea, took out her diary and made notes about her unusual experience in the antique shop. As she did so, she let her imagination take flight, picturing a scenario in which she lit the lamp's woollen wick and carrying it before her, used it to illuminate dark passages leading underground towards sinister cellars…

Once home, she immediately began to twist a woollen wick in anticipation of darkness falling. She then filled the lamp with animal fat, inserted the wick and lit the lamp. The wick burned surprisingly smoothly and was bright enough to lighten up the dark room; she was immediately entranced by its effect.

A chilly, autumnal wind drummed mercilessly on her windows, changing its rhythm with every fresh gust. Throwing on a waterproof, and protecting the flame with her hand, she took the lamp out to the garden behind her house.

Closing her eyes, she tried again, to imagine what people from past generations might have seen by the light of this lamp. A strong wind was blowing and the rain continued to pour. At one point she thought she caught a glimpse of a dark silhouette of someone wearing a hood pulled down low and shuddered at the notion that someone was watching her from behind the ivy-covered wall. With growing fear, she tentatively peered into the gloom but seeing nothing, relaxed a little, convincing herself that it had just been a figment of her imagination, undoubtedly triggered by her recollection of the stranger standing beside Mrs. Jane McKendry as she was leaving Centre.

After that, Miss J.M. did not linger in the garden for long and besides, after being battered by the wind and rain, the smoking wick began to emit a very unpleasant smell of burning wool.

Back inside, she lit the fire, heated up with a little glass of milk and placed the now extinguished lamp on her coffee table next to a cassette recorder. Warm again, she settled down to listen once more to a voice from her past, which spoke of events of long ago. Thus immersed, she found herself transported to somewhere far, far away.

The recording had been made in her youth shortly after she had received a tape recorder for her birthday. Years had passed and now the story of her ancestors, voiced by her dear grandfather, provided a unique opportunity for her to access important information which would benefit both her own research and areas of historical science on which she worked at the LMR. It was only now that she fully appreciated and understood the value of this special gift which had emerged, almost by accident, on that one occasion when her beloved grandfather had indulged his favorite granddaughter by agreeing to speak into the microphone of her new toy.

What had begun as a game, a childhood interest, had now become her life's work.

"The clue to the mystery should be a medallion containing a transparent stone ... This medallion, when lit in a specific way, either by lamp or candle, creates a spotlight effect which will reveal a sequence of secret signs" instructed the voice on the cassette. "Follow the message revealed by these signs and you will receive answers to all your questions."

She stopped the tape and tried to visualize those instructions she had already heard so many times. Allowing her mind to wander over the events, the people, and their destinies that emerged from the uncomplicated narratives of her grandfather, she then mentally drew up an action plan for the documentation of the images and characters that inhabited his stories.

Turning to the silver lamp, she carefully examined the patterns on both sides. The lamp was surprisingly heavy and had to be held with both hands. Its handle, when pressed at symmetric positions on either side of the bowl, slid backwards into the body to an indented section which appeared at some point to have been flooded with ink. This object must therefore have served as both a lamp and an inkwell. What else was there? J.M. was certain that some connection existed between this lamp, her grandfather's tales and very possibly, the mysterious fire at the church on Lauriston Road. But what was it? Hmm.

"Tomorrow I'll definitely have to look through the archives with Dr Silver. I'll tell him about the magical shop, show him the lamp and I'm sure that he will be able to break the spell and provide a convincing explanation of what happened today." J.M. flicked away a lock of hair which had fallen over her tired eyes.

Instinctively, she felt certain that every element of the narrative of the white-bearded elder Toktogul was of crucial importance, and in an effort to work out a reason, she now tried to focus on each aspect of his tale in graphic detail. The only way to achieve her aim was to methodically follow the clues along a small but infinite chain of facts and inferences, illuminating one secret after another…

Yet again, she turned her gaze to the lamp sitting before her.

Next morning, having taken some strongly brewed tea with two teaspoons of honey to brace herself against the cold, damp weather, she collected her documents and the package containing the silver lamp and headed for the city library where Doctor Brandon Silver anxiously awaited her. He intended to interrogate her about the life of the Russian author Mikhail Lermontov. To his astonishment and satisfaction, this was one of her most beloved Russian classical authors, and she was well acquainted with his biographical details, including the story of his great grandfather, who after fighting as a mercenary for the Swedes, was taken prisoner at Poltava and then spent the rest of his life in Russia.

"How interesting all of this is, especially since we'll soon be receiving tourists and colleagues who are fascinated by this poet! I've already sought out all of the necessary documents from the archive so that we'll have something to work on during the seminar." Doctor Silver proudly showed his assistant copies of the vintage records that he had made from originals in the city archive the previous day.

"That's just fantastic, doctor," responded J.M. readily. She was always inspired by the tremendous enthusiasm of this man, and his professional approach to things. Then, after a pause and with a degree of trepidation, informed him:

"Yesterday I bought an antique."

"What was it?" Doctor Silver's ears immediately pricked up. "I hope you can tell me?" He savoured his coffee and, smiling serenely, waited for her to continue.

"Of course, dear Doctor, that's why I brought it with me," she replied with a smile, and revealed the lamp.

"My God, what an unusual piece, quite extraordinary!" muttered the doctor, carefully turning the lamp one way and another.

"Yes, it is, isn't it, Doctor!" J.M agreed. She finished her tea and, placing her cup on the table, awaited his verdict with growing excitement.

"Where did you manage to get your hands on this?" The doctor straightened his glasses and narrowed his eyes, quite lost in thought.

"Yesterday I happened upon a very strange antique shop. I don't know how I ended up there: it was as though I had been was led there by some invisible force! Anyway, when I went in, my attention was immediately drawn to this lamp and I just had to buy it! I don't know why! I had a long conversation with the very knowledgeable and amenable dealer and he has promised to send me details about the piece from his archives." There was a tremor in her voice and she nervously tugged at one of her curls as she answered the Doctor.

"Perhaps we can try to work out how the lamp got here. After all, we now have access to an exhaustive archive of registration journals, spanning centuries, of logs of artefacts brought into Edinburgh by missionaries and traders from the Continent.

"Excuse me, Doctor! Could we assume that this silver lamp might not have come from Europe, but from somewhere much further away? If so, perhaps a more in depth study may lead me to answers that I have been seeking for a long time." J.M. quietly awaited his response.

"Why yes, would your request by any chance, be linked to what you've told me about some work that you've been doing on some recordings, and your mention of a rather unusual story? Perhaps the time has come for you to share some of the details with me?" The Doctor looked at her quizzically. "By the way, didn't you also say that you know a historian who recently travelled to Kyrgyzstan?" Ordering another cup of strong coffee, he searched through his laptop for a while. As someone who worked in historical science, as well as applied branches such as genealogy, Dr Silver had always shown great interest in the history of Central Asia.

"Doctor Silver," J.M. gently interrupted his deep concentration on whatever had captured his attention on his computer.

"What? Oh… Sorry," he triumphantly turned his laptop towards her to display a copy of archived registration documents which indicated that in the late sixteenth and early seventeenth centuries, well before the fire, merchant ships had arrived in Edinburgh from Turkey, bringing with them, a wide variety of goods from Central Asia, sourced from countries on the Great Silk Route, in Asia, Africa and Indochina…

Totally absorbed by their work, they hadn't noticed that night had fallen and the city was now awash with the gleam of electric light.

"Let's continue this at the Centre," suggested J.M., whose temple was throbbing with excitement. Gathering everything up from the table, they ordered a taxi and rushed to the door of the library. On reaching the Centre they rang the doorbell and waited impatiently for the massive door to open.

"Good evening, my dear Mrs Jane McKendry," Dr Silver greeted the Centre's watchwoman with a playful wink.

"Why so late?" muttered Mrs McKendry. She had been about to close the Centre, not expecting latecomers, and now glared at them with undisguised irritation.

J.M. automatically glanced at the corner where yesterday she had seen the suspicious stranger in the dark cloak.

"Why are you looking over there? Have you lost something, Miss J.M.?" asked Mrs McKendry unpleasantly.

Ignoring this comment and gently relieving her of the Centre's enormous key, Dr Silver tactfully advised: "Good evening to you, my dear. Please don't worry about anything! We will close up the Centre ourselves and even wash our own dishes!" He guided Mrs McKendry to the entrance and closed the creaking door behind her.

A strange feeling always came over J.M. when entering the old building at dusk. The half- light seemed particularly contusive to visions of phantoms, firing up her overactive imagination to such an extent that she could almost become dizzy. That happened all too often: the picturing of links between the past and the present. Oh, if only it were possible to recreate first hand, an accurate account of things that occurred in the past but continue to have an impact today!

More than ever, J.M. wished she could interact with the residents of old Edinburgh and especially those from this part of the city and the church, which had played such a large role in the lives of both locals and visitors.

How alluring and interesting! Dreams, dreams…

"Right, let's start. Here are the old documents relate to all the ships that called at Edinburgh's port during its rapid development as Scotland's trading centre, from 1621, around the time when the ban on thatched roofs was enforced, through to the beginning of the 17ᵗʰ century. The lists contain information on merchandise imported from Scandinavia, the Baltic, Western Europe, Africa and Asia but they also detail the names of the passengers and descriptions of their own, valuable possessions. We even have instructions and requests made and initialed by some of the passengers." Wearing white gloves, Dr Silver carefully turned the pages, studying the text with the assistance of a huge magnifying glass.

Finally, without raising his eyes from the old ledger, he asked to have another look at the silver lamp.

Dr Silver carefully began to examine the lamp and after a short while, gleefully announced that he had found initials similar to those in the ancient tome's records: very fine letters embossed at the very base of the silver lamp.

"We can see clearly the inscription: 'Ivan IV' but the numerals are blurred. However, I've found something else in the ledger which relates directly to the importation of this lamp! There's an instruction in Latin which reads 'May this creation find its master and may it bring him to the place where the holy path awaits,' followed the letters: 'Daria, daughter of Ivan IV'!"

"What unbelievable luck! It's astonishing! All this time I've so carefully yet unsuccessfully, looked for what I needed in the records, missing only the last tiny thread that could connect the past to the present!" Enthusiastically, opening the book at her side and borrowing Dr Silver's magnifying glass, J.M. in turn began to examine the mysterious initials at the base of the silver lamp, carefully noting them down in her journal.

They sat for a long time, trying to make sense of what they had just discovered and how it related to J.M's own story.

"We'll take a break, Miss J.M., sit down," invited Dr Silver, pouring himself a glass of whisky and offering one to his assistant, who had risen from her chair. After a couple of sips, J.M. resumed her examination of the text on the silver lamp and in the ledger, transferring both these and her notes to her laptop. They were both intoxicated by the excitement of what had been revealed and Dr Silver leaning back in his chair, waited eagerly for J.M. to finish her notes and begin her story…

Chapter III

The Birth of Kara-Choro

The land of gardens ascends to the horizon
Bearing a light to the sky
Gnarled crowns brown the contours,
Painted with branches on the horizon.
And the travellers down from the mountains are tired…
But now, having entered the flourishing land,
Watch, as down from valleys far,
The snow flowers will fly in silence.

Tash Miyashev. Translation from Kyrgyz by M. Smelnikov

This story dates back to the mid-16th century, in the city of Fergana. Peri-kana or Fergana literally translates as 'beautiful city' or 'city of angels'. The city of Fergana, located on the ancient Silk Road, has always been regarded as a heavenly place and mere words can barely describe its beauty. With its majestic nature, gardens and oases, it was a popular resting place for caravans making their way across Central Asia, attracting travellers from as far afield as India, China, Ancient Russia and Europe.

The smell of fruit: sundried grapes and prunes, apples and berries charged the air, a manifestation of the generosity and wealth of nature...

From morning until late in the evening the region's locals harvested. Women spread out large woven cotton cloths set about slicing the apples gathered by the children, whilst men, young and old, split ripe, juicy and sweet tasting apricots in half and laid them out in the yard to be dried by the warm and gentle autumnal sun. These traditional preparations for the winter performed in the early autumn as the trees slowly changed colour, and nature appeared to be bathed in gold, had its own special flavour and character. Lush maroon vine leaves whispered a quiet, magical melody and ripe grapes swayed gently like oriental dancers. This was a time when nature and people worked in perfect harmony.

After a full day's work, everyone tucked into tasty, ripe melons, which melted in the mouth like honey, and savoured the intoxicating scent of the hot, round flatbreads as they emerged, freshly baked, from tandoori ovens. After dinner, everyone pleasantly tired from their endeavours, prepared to sleep...

On one such evening, a full the moon appeared in a sky scattered with numerous stars which busily twinkled as if in silent conversation with each other. A fine thread of cloud, with gracefully undulating tentacles, as fine as a spider's web, passed across the bright moon, but other, more robust clouds formed figurative shapes and it was in these, that local elders sought good omens on which they invited the community to make wishes.

"Oh, oh, oh, ah, help me!" moaned an exhausted twenty-five year old woman. In severe pain form her second hour of labour, her eyes shone brighter than blackcurrants after summer rain and her lips, bitten to blood, were the colour of poppies that bloomed in May. Her contractions had begun earlier that day whilst she had been preparing a large samovar of tea for the boys from a neighbouring yard. At the time, she did not pay these twinges much attention since she had been told that she would only give birth after the harvest. Women from the village had arrived in the yard and were busy preparing a little fire on which to heat water next to the tapchan, the raised platform commonly used throughout Central Asia during the summer months for relaxing, eating and sleeping.

From time to time, the women comforted her by stroking her belly with a warm cotton rag and urged her to breathe deeply and try to relax. Their presence was reassuring and gave the young woman a degree of

confidence but the person who the young woman really wanted beside her, was the woman who served as the local healer.

"Oh! Oh! Help! Help! Where is our dear Healer?! Didn't you call for her ages ago?!" The weary woman looked anxiously around her.

"Hold on, sweet Tomchi:[1] be patient. They say that many women are giving birth in the neighbouring villages as well! There are lots of children being born this full moon; it's wonderful! This only happens once every twenty or thirty years!

"Push, Tomchi, push!" exhorted her middle-aged neighbour and with slender fingers, she gently stroked Tomchi's temples in a light soothing massage.

Twelve year old Dastan was a mischievous red-haired boy with cunning eyes, who constantly hiding from his parents, did not give them a moment's peace. Dressed today in a thin white shirt and wearing a hat on his head, he ran into the yard to announce the good news.

"Tomchi, our Healer is on her way. My father, Kanatbek, rode over to the next village to collect her: They'll be here any moment!"

Soon voices could be heard and a group of people rode into the courtyard on horseback. Among them was an older woman with a particularly loud voice, calling "I'm coming… I'm coming!"

The Healer dismounted from her horse, holding a cup of burning juniper and muttering something at the same time. Splendid in a sparkling clean maasy, with her head covered by a voluminous white scarf, and flat boots on her feet, this majestic woman with flashing eyes and an unusual birthmark under her left eye, commanded universal respect. It was said that she was a descendant of those who had miraculously escaped from a reign of tyranny in distant countries, forcing them to wander homeless for months and years until they stopped and settled in these parts…

"Move away from Tomchi! All of you! The local women dispersed as

---

1 *Tomchi: morning dew*
2 *Kara-Choro: Black warrior*

instructed and the Healer moving towards Tomchi, quietly repeated: "Oh Almighty, help this infant to be born healthy on this wondrous night! Suf! Bismillah!"

"Now, Tomchi, my dear: look at me and push harder. Placing a little opium under her tongue, she advised "Bismillah, this local medicine will help. You won't feel any pain and the scent of the smouldering juniper which I've brought along will soothe you. My hands will slowly pass across your stomach and you must then push as hard as you can!"

"Ah! Ah! Aaaaah!" With her pain alleviated, Tomchi mustered together all of her remaining strength to give an almighty push.

"I can see the head, and now the shoulders have appeared! Just one last push, Tomchi!" exhorted the Healer loudly.

And suddenly everyone was silenced by the heartening cry of a new life!

"Tomchi, it's a boy! What happiness: a boy is born!" cried the women with joy.

The Healer held the new-born in her arms.

"Oh Almighty, Oh Holy Umay-ene, thank you for your assistance," the Healer continued her prayer.

"Tomchi, we will place the child on your breast and he will remember your smell, his mother's smell, forever!" the Healer's eyes shone with delight.

The boy cried loudly, and his reddened nose poked at his mother's body, searching and taking in its smell.

"What will you call him, Tomchi?" asked the women.

Exhausted and weeping with happiness, Tomchi prayed to thank the Almighty and whispered something in her baby's ear. Everyone fell into a tender silence.

"His father asked that his son be called Kara- Choro,"[2] replied Tomchi eventually.

"Welcome to our world, Kara Choro!" Carefully washing him in warm water and cutting his umbilical cord, the Healer wrapped him in a white swaddling cloth…

Kara-Choro, smacking his lips, fed at his mother's breast. His voice was loud, but he rarely cried.

"Oh, look at his hazel eyes! And he has dark skin like his mother," whispered Tomchi's neighbour, as she helped swaddle the baby.

Following a tradition practiced in all corners of Central Asia for centuries, Tomchi's neighbour and the Healer did not go home until Tomchi had fully recovered, and mother and child did not appear in public for forty days after the birth. These forty days were considered special; a time when all of the child's guardian angels delivered their wishes for his good health and success.

Finding the Holy Path

***

Years race past without a backward glance,
Mother is inseparable from her baby.
In the spring, in the colours of black cherry,
The voice in the song is in tune.
In the summer mother takes her son fishing
Teaches him by a rapid stream...
The boy grew to everyone's joy
Helping the elderly,
Cutting grass in autumn,
Making roofs for the elderly,
Getting restless,
His nickname is glorious lad.
His black eyebrows blinking
A great mischief-maker
Then came the spring festival
Something is wrong with the local children
Here you see great discord
Everyone rushing around quickly
Gathered at the ditch,
There, the boys quarrelled,
The noise they made had a purpose...

***

Chapter IV

"Tell me, Mother, where is my Father?"

It was a beautiful, warm spring day. These were the days when every community celebrated the spring festival, Nooruz, and women dressed up in their brightest and newest clothes; beautifully patterned velvet chapans, worn over light Atlas dresses. The festival marked the start of a new season. According to both Central Asian tradition and the ancient druidic system, the arrival of spring occurred when the duration of both day and night was absolutely equal: the equinox.

It is said that on this day, at the beginning of time, the Gods went down to a river to drink its crystal-clear water, and one of them in boundless admiration uttered: new stream, new hopes, new day and new start... Nooruz! And nowadays this term is used for the spring festival throughout Central Asia.

The white-winged angels that hovered around the Gods presented them with trays for prayers and blessings for the New Year. The trays held seven items that in the Persian alphabet, all began with the letter 's', such as *sumolek, a* sweet drink made from germinated wheat seeds. The trays contained herbs, vinegar, wheat and barley, along with mirrors, candles and painted eggs. All of these items had symbolic meanings: the candle represented light or fire to protect people from evil spirits, while eggs and mirrors were needed to complete the old year and meet the first day of the new.

Spring is the time when people habitually review and change their expectations for a better life and so it was fitting that this holiday was set at the time when nature, in this magical region of Fergana, awoke from the dead, dark winter with the flowering of cherry and apple trees, the intoxicating smell of new, green meadow grass and the rush of life-giving, crystal-clear streams. The land in these parts was famous for its fertility and lovingly nurtured by its people, Nature responded bountifully.

The weather was wonderful, uplifting the souls of everyone in the community.

Children playing together on the narrow and dusty streets often fell out with each other. This was an important part of growing up since in arguments, one often finds truth. Young and innocent, the children were not yet accomplished in telling lies and they also had much to learn about sparing each other's feelings.

On this particular occasion, the boys had quarrelled over a game of bones.[3] Kara-Choro had retreated to a corner where he sat huddled, nursing a grudge against his peers. Strong-willed, he had once again been excluded as a result of his short temper and excessive use of physical force. He had no intention of apologising and had nothing to say in his defence.

"But it's just a game! Why doesn't anyone want to play by my rules? It's so simple," he later reasoned to adults who had been drawn by the noise of the children's disharmony.

"Mum! First, he started tricking us and then he took the hats (doppys), that we'd only just been given!" cried the red-haired boy, pointing at Kara-Choro. Cunningly, and out of sight of the adults, he then threw a fistful of sand right into Kara-Choro's eyes.

"Ow! That was sore! You always play too roughly and don't follow the rules," shouted Kara-Choro, rubbing his eyes and sobbing loudly.

Kara-Choro stood in a corner feeling peeved that the adults had become involved in this insignificant quarrel. His eyes were now red and heavily swollen by the sand which he tried to rub away with his shirtsleeve. It was not however, just the sand which caused his tears. He was being driven to despair by the boys constantly calling him "fatherless" it was this which had impelled him to retaliate by taking their new hats and throwing them into the nearest small spring.

---

3 Bones is a common game, like dominoes

"What a rascal you are!" exclaimed the Healer, the wise woman of the village. She was always attired in the traditional dress of the region, from the close-fitting silk handkerchief and second covering of white cotton on her head, to the trousers beneath her Atlas dress, and her narrow-toed mule boots embroidered with gold ribbon.

She knew all the locals, who had settled where and when, as well as everything else that went on, and her advice was sought by many people, even travellers. Her comprehensive knowledge of local traditions and customs gave her unique wisdom which she passed on to the new generation through all sorts of legends and fairy tales. How could the Healer, famous for her special gifts and her presence at the births of most of the local children, not have recognised the real reason for this little boy's angst?

Taking him by the hand, she smiled and led him firmly away, saying: "Let's go, my dear, to the nearest spring. We need to wash off all this sand and dirt and then I'll take you to your mum. And don't go bothering her with complaints about what happened in the yard. A game is a game."

On the way home, Kara-Choro glanced at her steady gaze but didn't say anything in return to the Healer.

"Right, Tomchi, I've brought your son home. He's been quarrelling again with the boys from the next street," The Healer related Kara-Choro's mischief with a smile, as she sat on the round platform and drank green tea.

"Thank you, dear Healer for bringing him back, as always. What am I to do with this rascal to stop him behaving like this?!" Tomchi lowered her eyes in embarrassment.

"Don't be upset and try not to scold him too much. Kara-Choro has a strong will, and the destiny that awaits him is not easy. You had better go and talk to him quietly; he's really a clever boy." Standing by the gate against the setting sun, the two women lingered for a few moments to share memories and secrets about their neighbours and other gossip.

Finally it was time for Tomchi to bid her guest farewell: Thank you again, Healer; bless you. Do come again! I'm always glad to see you!

As soon as the gate had closed, Kara-Choro approached his mother with sad eyes. "Mum, please could you ask one of the house-keepers to cook me a corn cob over the smouldering fire?"

"Very well, Kara-Choro."

Tomchi, whose brightly coloured robe embroidered with flowers reflected her cheerful disposition, suspected nothing as she headed into the yard. She asked one of the house-keepers to kindle the fire and cook sweetcorn for her son.

"Here you are," said Tomchi happily, as she brought through the hot corn on a tray.

"Mum, could you please pass it into my hands with your palms? asked Kara Choro, in a serious tone of voice.

Surprised by this unusual request, Tomchi picked up the hot cooked sweetcorn in her palms, but as she held it out to her son , Kara-Choro roughly grabbed ,then clasped, her hands together and loudly beseeched her, with tears in his eyes:

"Mum, tell me, where is my father? Tell me please, I beg you!" and he continued to hold his mother's hands tightly.

"Ow, my son, my hands are burning! Let me go! I'll tell you, I'll tell you! Let me go, please, Kara-Choro!" cried Tomchi.

Hearing her shout, neighbours rushed into the yard. The first was Kanatbek with his wife Saadat. They saw that Tomchi, both of whose hands were now immersed in cold water, was trying to tell her son something.

"What happened, Tomchi?!" asked Kanatbek in a frightened voice, staring at the mother and her son, who were sitting in the yard on the round platform.

A few moments later, he understood the essence of the situation, realising that Kara-Choro had asked her about his father, Tagay-bii.

Patting the boy on his back, he told him that he himself would tell him everything tomorrow morning, when they climbed on the roof to meet the sunrise. Then, wishing Tomchi and her son sweet dreams, he returned home with his wife.

The next morning, sitting on the roof of the house and looking at the twelve year old son of his best friend Tagay-bii, Kanatbek began his story. They drank natural yogurt made from cow's milk with added water and salt, to ward off the heat of the sun.

Kara-Choro listened to Kanatbek carefully, staring at him with rising astonishment.

At this age boys, on the cusp of manhood, commonly look for heroes to emulate and formulate in their minds, people in whom they can place their trust and with whom they can share secrets too intimate to ever be revealed to parents, best friends or neighbours.

So Kara-Choro chose to confide in Kanatbek, a kindly man and who, always ready to offer wise advice, had become a sort of guardian angel.

Kanatbek was then 65 years old and it was believed that he had been settled in the area for exactly twelve years!

They say that he was the closest and most loyal friend of one of the most important *biis*[4] in the northern regions, where the sun first rises. It was not for nothing that Kara Choro sought him out so early in the morning on the roof of the house to meet the sunrise.

In the steppes that bordered the northern regions, Kanatbek once had a family. Then Dzungars[5] captured all of his Lesser Horde. They say he miraculously escaped and ran to the place where he met and faithfully served his new people: the Northern Khan.

---

4 *Bii's – clan chiefs*

5 *Djungars – represented by multinational group of tribes and people. Between the Volga and Dunay rivers, located in the Eastern European territory there was a mixture of tribes: the Kimmerissy, Skifs, Sarmats, Gunns, Pechenegs and Polovs.*

***

Kanatbek told Kara-Choro about the evil Dzungars whose quest it was to burn and destroy any form of life that got in their way. He described how he and his Horde had been a bulwark in the fight against the evil spirits that possessed their enemies.

Because of their reputation, Kanatbek and his Horde had for many years, been commissioned to accompany valuable cargo being transported from one territory to another. Famous for protecting the interests of innocent people, they became known as the "White Warriors of the Desert": defenders of trade routes.

Their assistance was particularly valued by the caravans who faced great risks of losing their goods to ruthless Dzungars and other dark forces as they traversed the lonely and seemingly endless steppes of Central Asia and the territory of Great Russ.

With strong connections with the Golden Horde, the caravans' cargoes included priceless manuscripts from Roman rulers, medical secrets of Egyptian pharaohs, and writings from the ancient inhabitants of Scandinavia. The "Silk Road" had an unquestionable impact not only on trade in the immediate region, its political stability and social and economic growth, but also, upon the development of world trade.

When Kanatbek arrived at Tagay-Bii's Khanate, his language differed from that of the locals: he used words that sounded softer than the local dialect of northerners. It was said he was a good military adviser. But it was as though his kind, narrow eyes were always searching for something left behind in his native land; his gaze was turned to the past. He was thoughtful and taciturn; a wise and sensitive man of nobility who had the gift of restoring calm whenever turbulent situations arose.

It is said that the most abhorrent enemy is someone in whom you once placed your trust, and Kanatbek had first-hand experience of this when a Dzhungar betrayed him in order to steal his pastures. The

Dzhungar had appeared on his land in the rags of a dervish, accompanied by a red-haired, overweight and thick-lipped woman, who people secretly believed to be an evil witch. One evening she brewed a potion which she served to Kanatbek's warriors, rendering them powerless in the defence of the whole army of Dzungars who attacked the next morning...

Kanatbek, suspecting nothing, had already left his family and pastureland to go hunting. On the way he stumbled across his neighbour Baatyrzhan who wounded and bleeding, was hiding with his wife and new-born baby in a cave. They had managed to escape from barbarism of the man that had been Kanatbek's guest and whom he had treated as one of his family, giving him shelter and land.

Baatyrzhan told Kanatbek that the stranger to whom he had entrusted his pasture and family, had seized everything that morning, mounting his attack with a horde of Dzungars, and that he now intended to hunt down Kanatbek and hang him without trial or mercy!

After the attack in which the warriors had been slain and the land successfully seized, the bodies of those murdered had been taken to a tent and brutally burned in front of the women, children and elderly.

"What about my family? What happened to them?" yelled Kanatbek, unable to comprehend the terrible series of events being told by his neighbour.

"Your wife resisted the Dzungars to the end! Hearing about how they were burning those wounded warriors she ran into the tent, but overcome by the smoke, was killed alongside them," Kanatbek's mortally wounded neighbour, now wheezing and struggling to breathe, looked at him with beseeching eyes, and continued:

"Kanatbek, I've always been a loyal friend to you and now, as I face death, I ask you a favour! Please bring up my precious son, Dastan as your own. Love my wife as your own. Flee, flee to the north! Ride to the Khanate of Tagay-bii. Take this camel. It is strong and will be able to outpace your pursuers. Let the Almighty show you the way... Leave me here; my wounds are fatal. One blow from a Dzungar spear, and I fell to the ground: my life is finished. Kanatbek, what I have witnessed today, sadly proves that human cruelty, jealousy, betrayal and evil know no bounds! More than anything in my life, I am thankful for my son: Cherish him!" He made to take a sip of the water Kanatbek had brought, but exhausted, and toppling backwards, Baatyrzhan breathed his last.

Kanatbek's heart was consumed with anger and despair. He clutched Baatyrzhan tightly and, lifting his tear struck face to the sky, he said bitterly:

"Oh Almighty, give us strength, give us clean air! Tomorrow is another day and again the lark will be singing in the sky! May my friend rest in peace, let the hero sleep his eternal sleep on Kazakh land! Omin!"[6]

After covering his friend's body with stones and saying his prayer, Kanatbek tied his horse to the camel and left immediately with Saadat, Baatyrzhan's widow, and son for the North. Saadat sat behind him, hugging Dastan and clinging to the camel's large hump. Covered with dust, she was trembling with shock, but dared not shout or cry, because Dzungars were already in pursuit. They say that Saadat was silent for many days and months and never said a word. Only at night did she cry at the river, thinking about her husband Batyrzhan...

***

You're in my heart, we breathed as one...
I live and carry two lives
Your spirit is with me everywhere
O Batyrzhan – you're mine forever...
May our tender nights remain in my dreams,
You are the little sparrow,
That jumped and hopped today in the meadows
I see you everywhere, and in my dreams...

Kanatbek adopted his friend's wife Saadat and son Dastan as his own, and supported them in every respect.

It was said that when they arrived in the northern region, they were met by local people to whom they related details about their escape from their native Kazakh steppe.

Having heard the story, angry Tagay-bii ordered that Kantabek and his new family be given a yurt, a plot of land and their own fiefdom.

Tagay-bii was recognised for his generosity and his pastures were grazed by countless herds of the best horses, which in turn, provided his people with the most delicious fermented mare's milk in these parts.

And there they remained, in the homeland of their new lord and protector, and gradually they assimilated with the local people and learned their customs. Although well settled in the community, they were not immune to local gossip. Many whispered that Saadat was not in fact, Kanatbek's wife at all but his sister: the couple behaved too chastely with each other, even when they believed they were alone. Such stupid rumours always reached Kanatbek, but he paid no attention to them.

The rumours and opinions of locals didn't bother Saadat either. Together they brought up the boy with love, and the red-haired boy with mischievous eyes reciprocated this.

Kanatbek never left his wife and son alone. He even took Saadat with him when he went hunting, and taught her how to shoot from a bow. Kanatbek tied a sturdy belt around his chest, and wrapped it around Dastan, and thus, they remained inseparable. Such hunting trips were Kanatbek's way to relax and unwind, as he tried to preserve his human dignity despite the situation. He wanted to reteach Saadat how to love life, and to accept him as her new husband. These efforts stopped Kanatbek retreating into himself and dying from grief for his homeland.

He was patient…

---

6 *Omin- Amen.*

One fine night, when Dastan was fast asleep, Saadat, untying her hair, quietly awoke Kanatbek and whispered in his ear that he leave the yurt.

The new moon loomed fine with graceful contours, symbolising the beginning of a new cycle, a new month.

The warm air was filled with the sound of crickets and the gurgling of a waterfall and the velvety sky studded with bright, twinkling stars made the night feel enchanted and magical.

Saadat had never looked so beautiful. Her gaze wavered as if to avert painful memories, her eyes filled up with unshed tears and her lips trembled with unspoken words.

"I had a dream, Kanatbek! The sparrow that sang today near our yurt was the soul of my husband. And he was saying: 'Live for both us! Live, Saadat. Do not grieve and do not cry for me!'"

The tears that she had been unable to shed for so long flooded out that night! Trembling, she held Kanatbek tight, and her lips touched those of her new husband…

They covered each other with tender kisses, talking to each other about love, and about the beauty and preciousness of life.

Kanatbek caressed Saadat, but now her tears were of newfound and unconditional happiness. Beside her was her saviour, her hero, the man who had accepted and brought up her Dastan like his own son.

"Kanatbek, take me, love me: I will be true to you and will be with you forever!

They clung to each other in a burst of tender and passionate love, and their ardour blazed like fire in the warm summer night. They felt as though they had been reborn and that everything around them had stopped still, as they entered paradise. Kanatbek, who had waited long for this moment, clenched his strong arms around Saadat. Their bodies merged, like two streams flowing into one large river. Dazed, they continued to whisper words of love and tenderness. It was a moment of pleasure to be remembered forever.

"Saadat, Saadat! … You are all that remains of my homeland! You and Dastan are everything that reminds me of where I come from and who I am. You are the reason I keep breathing; my spirit, my strength and my weakness. Saadat: if I didn't have you in my life, I would have drowned long ago and couldn't have survived. In you is the strength of our home, the strength of Khan Tengri. In you is the stream that we drank from, the bread that we baked: In you are my dreams and my future." He kissed her on her cheek and plunged his face between her lush breasts.

"Oh, my dear, forgive me for taking so long to come to you. Forgive me for making you wait. But now in your arms, I am reborn as a woman, a cherished and beloved woman all over again."

Afterwards, they spoke long, reminiscing about the steppe, and those they had left there. She was silent as he spoke and then, when she was moved to sing ancient songs of her homeland, he in turn became the listener.

***

One such passionate summer night they conceived a son, whose arrival would bring great affection and joy to Kanatbek and Saadat, and a younger brother for Dastan. They called him Daniyar.

***

Nine or ten years passed before a messenger arrived to call attendance at the next council meeting for all the biis of clans, large and small, of peoples living in Central Asia. This was an important gathering on a vast scale, which lasting many weeks, had enormous impact not only on the countries through which the Silk Road passed, but also, neighbouring countries and even powers as far afield as European Russ, China and Europe.

Kanatbek took along his family, Saadat, Dastan and Daniyar, as well as his warriors. They were accompanying the Kyrgyz Tagay-bii, whom he continued to serve faithfully. It is believed that the Kyrgyz bii had always remained loyally protective of Kanatbek, refusing large sums of money to hand him over to the Dzungars and certain death.

***

Central Asia served as a vast arena for incessant strife, wars, and attacks on caravans. Discussion on strategies to combat these problems and the instigation of laws to deal with them had to be undertaken in peace and harmony. After all, the paths of all peoples, whether Kyrgyz, Kazakh, Mongol, Djungar, Tatar, Uzbek, Uighur, Turkmen or Tajik, overlapped in this part of the territory, and the Silk Road had great economic and political importance for all their trade interests and welfare. The event also attracted Caravan-bashis from distant countries, including Turkey, India and Persia. On this occasion, the council meeting to be attended by delegations and ambassadors from throughout a vast geographical area was hosted by the Khan of Bukhara. Of urgent concern was the significant rise in merciless and murderous attacks by the ever- plundering and greedy Dzungars.

In addition to military and political spheres, the gathering was also an important forum for the biis and khans to discuss issues such as disputes concerning levels and collection of taxes from traders passing through different regions along the Silk Road, and as significantly, the sustenance and promotion of cultural traditions and heritage through the construction and maintenance of medressas, and the publication and spread of new philosophies of the imams and epic poems penned by the akyns.

Since a wide variety of languages was spoken by the delegations, the Gathering was mainly conducted in Uighur: the trade language of the

Silk Road and that used by all caravans to communicate with each other.

Tents and yurts were set up, creating a temporary city inhabited by the most eminent and influential political and military figures of the day supported by their community elders and well-populated entourages.

Leading the Kyrgyz delegation was Tagay-bii. They had travelled far, from the most northerly of their country where snow on the Ala Too range does not melt even in the summer, where snow leopards hunt mountain goats, where wild argali sheep climb the highest peaks and where glaciers generously irrigate the land with crystal clear water to provide the finest pastures.

Tagay-bii was described as being very tall, with light brown hair. The gaze of his grey-green eyes spoke of wisdom accrued both from life experience and from age-old knowledge and values passed down from his ancestors. He was celebrated as a skilled hunter, as cunning as a wild lynx, and in battles and duels, he had no equal. His selfless devotion to his country made him a profound and subtle politician, a figurehead of such stature that his life and achievements were well documented in historical records.

***

Tagay -bii was born around 1460 - 1470, in an area through which the River Iyrii Suu

Bylpyldak flows. This suggests that his birthplace was either in the south of Kyrgyzstan, in the Osh region, or

in Iyrii- Suu, in the Jayil district of the Chui region. Both areas shared the name of Iyrii suu, which translated from Kyrgyz, means "curved river".

According to reports, Tagay-bii was already middle aged when he resided in the court of Ereshe -Khan, prior to returning to his homeland. (B.Soltoev)

In the book " Tarikh- i - Rashidi", by Mohammed Hayder claims that Tagay-Bii was captured in battle with the head of the Mughals,Sultan Said Khan, on the Southern coast of Issik-kul at Barskoon. He was exiled to Kashgar, released in 1522 but then re-captured in 1524. He was held prisoner until 1533, when Sultan Said Khan died.

Tagay-bii ruled his people. He was second son of Ak-Uul("White son")and grandson of Dolon -Bii.

Evidence suggests that during a gathering for all the clans and in accordance with   ancient tradition,   Tagay-bii and his eldest brother, Adigin, divided power and land between them.   A rough boundary was created at the river Kara- Darya in the Osh region, with the higher northern part of the territory taken by Tagay-bii and the southwestern area given to Adigin.

Tagay-bii was a founder of the right wing(grouping) of clans, including the majority of the northern clans: Boke, Sarybagush, Solto, Bagysh, Sayak,

Chekir Sayak(Chekir-moldo, the blue eyed mullah) and Azyk.

Tagay-bii died between 1535 and 1540 but the legacy of his political activities continued into the late 17th and early 18th centuries.

The unification of the left and right wings of the political confederation covered the vast territory from Talas to Issy-Kul and Naryn.

Chapter V

The Meeting of Tagay- Bii and Tomchi of Bukhara

"Your image is like a delicate and tender east wind, as beautiful as the first snowdrop, the scarlet poppy of the Ala-Too, and as radiant as the first rays of sun at dawn. For many years it will sustain me and make it possible for me to realise the impossible." These were the words which Tagay-bii dreamt of reciting to the woman who would become the love of his life.

And here in Fergana, he was at last destined to meet her...

Tomchi had been raised at the court of the Bukharan Khan and her parents, good and noble people, had nurtured and rejoiced in her musical talents since she was young. And very soon, throughout the land, she became famed as much for her beauty, as her clear, melodic voice and virtuoso on the dutar.

Along with other local girls, Tomchi had been invited to the Central Asian council gathering to perform music on the dutar before the Khan's most important guests, including Tagay-bii.

At the end of the concert, it took but a few moments and one brief glance to impel the mesmerised Tagay-bii to address Tomchi, with words audible to only her.

"You are the one who destiny has sent me, the one for whom I've been waiting for so many years." Statuesque, Tomchi looked silently at Tagay-bii for several moments. Then she quickly retreated to the place where the other women were preparing huge pots of hot tea for the guests.

Left alone, Tagay-bii could only continue his declaration in his head. "Your gaze has struck me like lightning. Your body has tempted mine in my dreams, long before I set eyes on you. You are the one who causes my heart to tremble, the mistress of the dreams through which I have wandered all my adult life."

They had only shared a single glance but in spite of such a fleeting encounter and their age difference, Tagay-bii was already painfully aware that his feelings for this girl were real.

Tagay-bii had been in these parts many times and had travelled extensively. He had been in combat, and even in captivity, but had somehow always survived. In the arms of other wives and women, he had always felt as though there was someone from afar, who was smiling and waiting for him. Had he now have met her at last? Each time, he had considered this a fantasy; a way of dealing with the violence in his life. But now, he recognised that it had been a vision of what destiny had always had in store for him.

"It cannot be…" muttered Tagay-bii, closing his eyes and tilting his face skywards.

At that moment, his faithful friend Kanatbek appeared by his side.

"Tagay-bii! What is it that 'cannot be'? Tell me! I'm worried about you. Today's meeting is very important; are you all right? Are you ready to meet the Bukhara Khan? You've been preparing your speech for so long: surely you aren't having any doubts about its content?"

"I don't know what's wrong with me, Kanatbek my friend, I don't know. It may be that I am simply tired from the journey." Then, not wanting to reveal anything else, he turned his attention to their schedule concerning business and politics which had brought them here. "We must firstly go and greet my dear friend the Khan of Bukhara, and thereafter, over the next few weeks, focus on the reasons for our presence here. Just look at how many people have travelled here from all over Central Asia and beyond! We must ensure that our voice is heard and our missions accomplished. Kyrgyzstan will not be shamed." Speaking in a rich, baritone, Tagay-bii quickly regained his confidant composure, to dispel any feelings of anxiety expressed by Kanatbek.

As they set out to pay their respects to their host, the pair stopped to stare in wonder at the vast, arena of yurts and tents which provided temporary accommodation for thousands of delegates. Turbaned members of the caravans, with faces blackened by the sun and dust, and eyes languid with fatigue, were gathered by the river to water and wash their camels and to cleanse themselves after long and arduous journeys. Bathed in the scarlet rays of the setting sun, the scene epitomised the flavour of latter day paintings of ancient Arabia.

On the opposite side of the river, travellers had arrived from distant Persia. They would be spending some time here, resting their caravans, before crossing and continuing their long trek towards Europe.

The opulence of their goods: woven fabrics, carpets, silks, silverware, jewellery, spices, exotic dried fruits, medicines and intoxicating beverages spoke of multiculturalism and entrepreneurship which lay at the heart of this magical festival in the Fergana valley.

Tagay-bii made his observations with the detachment of a philosopher, but on a more emotional level, experienced heartfelt delight and enormous pride in everything around him.

Reaching the Khan's palatial residence with its blue dome and sparkling gold minaret, they were immediately surrounded by a multitude of servants dressed in white turbans and blue velvet coats embroidered with gold thread, carrying trays laden with a splendid spread of exotic dishes. Sitting in the centre of the hall, The Bukhara Khan welcomed everyone on arrival but as soon as he saw Tagay-bii, he rose to his feet and greeted him with a warm embrace.

"Oh my dearest and esteemed guest Tagay-bii, Khan of the northern Kyrgyz, welcome to my land!

"Assalam alleikum, Tagay-bii, son of Ala-Too the mountain from which rivers flow to quench my people's thirst; the land which turns to paradise in the spring and provides a feast in autumn; the land whose waters are the very sources of all life and which bring prosperity to our

cultivators! Tagay-bii: your presence here is the most precious to me."
Putting his hand to his chest, the Bukhara Khan ended his formal greeting
and they embraced again.

"Oh, alleikum assalam, my dear and mighty Khan of Bukhara,"
Tagay-bii greeted the ruler, in return.

After informal conversation and polite enquiries about the health
and welfare of the Khan's family, Tagay-bii excused himself on the pretext
of having to greet his own guests, and wearily retired to his voluminous
yurt, newly erected by his warriors and local labourers.

As was the custom, he was soon presented with a silver pot containing
warm water and a copper basin. It was delivered by Dastan, Kanatbek's
son: "Tagay-bii ata! I've brought you clean water so you can wash your
face and relax a little after the long and tiring road."

"Ah! Our little warrior Dastan! You must only be ten or eleven but
you're already so grown up! Thank you for your care and consideration
and thank your father for training you well!"

Rinsing his face, he reflected on how much he admired Kanatbek's
sensitive, parenting skills. His sons were brave and polite and since early
childhood, had strongly adhered to the traditional practice of always
treating their elders with the utmost respect. They also followed closely,
other local, and sometimes ancient, customs, thus keeping alive aspects of
the community's heritage which were a vital part of their identity.

"Go and tell my men that I would like some hot tea."

"Your wish is my command, Tagay-bii ata!" Dastan ran away from
the yurt with a mysterious glint in his mischievous eyes.

Less than three minutes later, someone did arrive with some tea but
instead of one of Tagay-bii's entourage it was someone wearing a silk
dress and silver necklaces which rustled and jangled as she entered the
yurt. The guard threw open the inner curtain, allowing the girl who was
carrying tray, on which sat a silver teapot and a small porcelain bowl, into
Tagay-bii's room. Bowing her head, she announced softly:

"Most esteemed Tagay-bii, Khan of the Northern Territories, your tea is ready!"

Disconcerted, Tagay-bii looked up to discover that standing before him, was the very same Bukharian beauty whom he had encountered earlier that day, gazing at him with eyes that sparkled like ripe blackcurrants. As if in the presence of an ethereal being, someone who had long haunted his dreams, he was momentarily, stunned into silence. She in turn, stood awkwardly, lowering her long dark lashes. Then sensitive to her feelings, Tagay-bii pulled himself together and invited Tomchi to come closer and serve the tea.

"Come and sit beside me, my beauty: I am dying of thirst! Tell me your name" Tagay-bii, asked softly.

"My name is Tomchi, most-esteemed Tagay-bii," she responded blushing, with eyes downcast.

"Your appearance is familiar to me, Tomchi. I beg you, do not be embarrassed. Let me see your face; you have beautiful eyes which could fire a man with love.

"Honourable Tagay-bii, my northern Khan, please excuse my indiscretion, but when I saw you my heart froze. I have heard much about you and your arrival here has been eagerly anticipated. It is said that you are a fine politician, very generous and fair, and excel in combat."

Tagay-bii, tried to conceal his fervour by leaning back on the cushions but as he reclined, the bowl of hot green tea, gifted to the Khan by the Chinese delegation, spilled over his silver-threaded brocaded robe.

Leaping to the rescue, Tomchi tried to wipe down his clothes, but since both his robe and shirt were soaked through, she suggested that he remove them so that she could dry the tea from his shoulders and torso. Tagay-bii didn't hesitate to do as she asked.

"Good God, how many scars and wounds you have!" exclaimed Tomchi, as she carefully helped him into fresh clothes. Whilst selecting theses garments from a chest in the corner of the room, she had come across his broad leather combat belt, embellished with intricately tooled patterns by master craftsmen, and had shuddered at the thought of all of the battles which he had endured.

Tagay-bii felt that he was living in a dream as Tomchi's delicate fingers involuntarily stroked his scars, as she dressed him.

"Is something wrong, Tagay-bii, my northern Khan? You've grown so silent; so deep in thought! What's wrong?" Tomchi suddenly feeling very self-conscious and embarrassed stepped away from her guest but as she did so, their eyes met and no words were needed to express the pure, sensual and ardent passion which they felt for one another. They waited longingly for dusk and the dark night which followed, when they could be together.

Tagay-bii and Tomchi were so passionately absorbed by each other that they failed to notice how the first rays of morning sun fell through the yurt's round roof, dancing on its beautiful felt roof embroidered with bright and graceful patterns.

Their spiritual love for each other continued through the following night to the first sunlight. They ran into the garden where, before sunrise under a blossoming apple tree, they spent magical time in each other's company. In the flowering apple trees the two lovers saw a divine and propitious sign. It seemed that in place of ordinary flowers, beautiful butterflies fell on their naked bodies, fluttering their wings. She bit her lips and moaned with pleasure and her eyes reflected the light of the stars which watched over the loving couple. These nights of love were not the first either for him or for her. He eagerly and skilfully kissed her erect nipples, and caressed her soft tanned body. His strong hands caressed Tomchi until she sweltered with desire, and the veins of the lovers' temples throbbed, merging with the rhythm of the cicadas signing at night.

Tagay-bii had never in his life, experienced such passionate and spiritual love but their union was to be short-lived since Tagay-bii's visit to the valley was already nearing its end and they might never again see or touch one another.

On one of these nights they conceived a child who, even if they were to be parted forever, would always embody their great love.

"Tomchi, my love, you have given me a new life! Now I know why destiny brought me on this trip to this valley. Indeed, Fergana is Peri-Kana! Tomchi, our child will be a gift from heaven! Sadly, I will soon be on my travels but I will leave my most faithful friend, Kanatbek, here with his family. Here is my hand made pocket knife with my initials. If the child is a girl, you must raise her yourself. But if it is a boy, call him Kara-Choro. When he turns sixteen, give him this pocket knife and send him on his way! If the Almighty is merciful, he will find me and continue my life's work. I will await news from you, Tomchi," said Tagay-bii.

"Oh, northern Khan, my eternal love! I could never love anyone else so passionately. I give you my word that if our child is a son, I will give him your knife and send him to you!" replied Tomchi, wiping away her tears at their parting.

"Dear Tomchi, my life does not belong to me! I have duties to my country and my people. Now, by agreement with the other biis and your Khan, I must do what has been agreed here: instigate new laws, so that we can continue to repel our enemies, and so my people and other tribes can live in peace and harmony." Clasping her tightly he tenderly, he said goodbye.

"I know that a special destiny has been ordained for you, Tagay-bii my northern Khan. I will pray for us and for our future!" With bitter tears and showering him with hot kisses, she parted from her beloved.

The stars twinkle silently
in the spectral garden
Magical nights
vanish with the first rays of sun
at the place where souls merge into a single stream,
flowing through the apple orchard that holds these secrets.
The love of Tagay-Bii and Tomchi builds bridges that will endure
centuries!
"My darling, I will retain your every breath
within me,
May all our secrets,
reveries and dreams, be stored
silently by the same moon that
was our witness!"
Clutching tightly at her breast, Tomchi
quietly watched Tagay.
"Dear Tomchi I waited with hope
for our meeting...
My soul will traverse centuries and epochs.
You are everything I was looking for in my dreams.
Our love will survive
all the trials of fate,
We will live forever,
Our souls in the stream of time,
will draw closer together, ever stronger.
Through ghostly dreams
I will run to you,
In your tender dreams
I'll come, if only once, to gaze
into your dark eyes...
We are forever, Tomchi!"

Tagay bade farewell:
With a flick of his whip
his steed galloped away...

Tomchi watched after him.
not once wiping her tears away.
"Gallop, Tagay, gallop...
We will be together forever,
and I will come to you in your dreams,
only to be
in your arms.
My love for you will bridge the ages!"

At the end of the conference, the Khan of Bukhara prepared a magnificent feast which lasted three days and three nights.

The Khan was a generous host: wine and fermented horse and camel's milk flowed freely and steaming platters of plov, the traditional dish of Central Asia, were flavoured with the distinctive rice and herbs of the region. The delegates guests were in good spirits, as much had been agreed in terms of laws and actions on trade and taxes which would benefit all of the inhabitants of Central Asia.

"Tagay-bii, one day everything decreed by this gathering will be recorded in history," said the Bukhara Khan happily to his special guest, seated to his right at the big round table. "May the scrolls that bear the chronicles of these events, negotiations and progress become legendary in the mapping of the future of these lands and their inhabitants. Nobody knows who will replace us or what sort of rulers will follow in the future. No-one knows what changes await us... But this congress will play a special role in history, as an example of how so many nations were able to reach harmonious agreements and wise decisions, for the common good of all of our people. May the Almighty himself be a witness to all that has happened! Omin! May Almighty Bless us all!" proclaimed the Khan of Bukhara, before giving his blessing to everyone present.

The evening ended with a spectacular cultural programme of traditional Eastern performances by the country's most esteemed singers, musicians, and swirling dervishes. Mostly travellers and story tellers, they lived through East to Persia.

A middle-aged, swarthy-skinned man with grey hair and bright blue eyes was accompanied by a flute as he sang a moving and epic ballad about the devastation of war and the forced, mass exodus of those who survived, to distant lands. He sang about the evil and pitiless deeds of the Dzungars, and their destruction of entire communities and the ancient cultural heritage of cities: acts which turned civilisations to dust. His sad song reminded all who listened of the fragility of human life and the importance of hope, faith, love and charity for peaceful and harmonious societies.

And as predicted by the Khan, records of this grand gathering, transmitted through oral history, poetry and prose, as well as formal documents, did indeed become legendary. They contributed to the rise and fall of the Golden Horde, added another rich layer to the region's social, economic and political history and as importantly, had a significant impact on relationships between Central Asia, Russia, Persia, Turkey and Europe for generations to come.

Chapter VI

"The Meeting of Kara-Choro and his Father Tagay-Bii"

"Well then, let's pray for a safe trip, Kara-Choro!" Kanatbek along with his wife Saadat and their two children Dastan and Daniyar, saddled their camels ready to accompany Kara-Choro on his long journey to finally meet his father, Tagay-Bii.

"The road is a long one; here, take this round flatbread, dried yogurt and apricots." Tomchi, restless and anxious about their imminent departure, pressed yet more provisions into their hands. Unable to leave her country, she could only hope that God would bless the travellers so dear to her, with a safe journey.

"Mum, I promise to send news via passing caravans. I beg you: please don't worry too much!" Saying farewell, Kara-Choro embraced his mother tightly.

"Ride through the pass", advised the elderly village Healer, who had also come to say goodbye. "May the Almighty show mercy on the wayfarers, and keep them safe from enemies! May they arrive in the north in one piece! Amen!"

With her blessing ringing in their ears, the travellers set off and were soon out of sight of their friends and neighbours who waved long after them, wiping away their tears.

***

On the journey, something wonderful and strange occurred: after two days and two nights making fair progress towards the north, they stopped at a place called Ichilik. Here they met boy, of about twelve or fourteen years old, who with great patience, was diligently tracking local partridges. The group asked him what had brought him here.

"I have been in these parts for quite a long time, trying to learn how to become a renowned hunter," replied the boy, squinting in wonder against the bright sun at their dusty faces.

"Where are you going?" noticing the dreamy and impetuous gaze of his peer, he addressed Kara-Choro directly.

"I'm going to meet my father. His name is Tagay-bii," answered Kara-Choro proudly.

"Are you here alone? Where are your people?" asked Kanatbek, noticing that the boy was carrying a large bag as well as his hunting equipment on his back.

"I ran away from my homeland long ago and am now living here by myself. I've been waiting for a caravan to come through before going any further since that's the only way I'll have any protection against the evil Dzungars. I'm thinking of heading towards Bukhara to serve the Khan," said the boy.

"Which Dzungars are these? Are they roaming these parts? Kanatbek-ata's eyes widened in amazement.

He suddenly realised that this boy could be one of those whose life fate had miraculously spared many years ago.

"Tell me, you were not, by any chance, a resident of the village that was captured after its warriors had been drugged by an old witch and then murdered by the Dzungars?"

"Yes, that was my village! Those who were able, fled at nightfall, whilst the Dzungars continued to assault the women, beat the elders, and put the children to work without food or rest," gasped the boy.

Kanatbek immediately dismounted his camel, embraced the boy and broke into tears of joy at the discovery that here was someone else from his small horde that was still alive.

"Oh God! And then what happened? Why did the villains leave?" Kanatbek asked impatiently, hardly believing his ears.

"The red-haired witch with big cheeks   loved the eldest Dzungar and said that she wanted to marry him. But he rejected her and she left the area, full of anger. Then a strange disease arrived, and all the Dzungar soldiers who ate from a single pot began to die, one after another. The Dzungar's leader was furious and in his rage, ordered that all those who had come into contact with the infected, be burned. It was his belief that the "black death" had been the work of the spurned witch. Many ran off to hide in the caves, and later they left the area completely," said the boy bitterly.

"So that's why the caravans travelling through that area haven't reported any attacks by the Dzungars for some time!"

Kanatbek could not believe what he was hearing, or that someone from his tribe was not only still alive but was now standing before him like a ghost from the past, telling this story...

"Oh, Khan Tengri, you have heard my prayers, evil always destroys itself! I thank the heavens, that here stands someone from my "little horde", he said, closing his eyes, and the travellers joined his prayer.

"And now, our friend, you must come with us. You are one of our people; let us protect you!" Kanatbek and Kara-Choro smiled happily as in unison, they invited the boy to join them.

As they continued their journey, they happened upon two other young men in a similar situation and they too, joined the group.

After the several weeks, they eventually arrived in the northern territories and were informed by the locals that Tagay-bii could be found on the summer pastures, at a place called Song Kol close to the high mountains which they could see in the distance.

Traversing a beautiful and abundantly fertile landscape, they stopped to spend a couple of nights with a nomadic family in their yurt. In return for such hospitality, the boys presented their hosts with some rabbits which they'd shot. The skins were retained to be sewn into warm hats whilst the meat, cooked in big pot, provided a wholesome meal. Afterwards, relaxing with beakers of mare's milk, the travellers shared tales of their journey, including accounts of the caravans they had met and through which Kara-Choro had, as promised, sent tidings to his mother and the Healer.

***

Weary, the group welcomed the coolness of the late summer days and as they rested, also enjoyed observing the cultural differences between the extended family with which they were staying and the people back home in the Fergana valley. Old and young women dressed quite differently to one another and while married women wore elegant *elecheks*[7] on their heads, unmarried women wore beautiful hats , decorated with bird feathers. The men wore white felt kalpaks, traditional hats embellished with elaborate embroidery, all year round.

In honour of the arrival of their guests from distant Fergana, the family dedicated and slaughtered a lamb which was allowed to cook slowly over the fire in a large cauldron to provide a rich broth and tender meat.

"Drink up the broth: there's plenty of it and it's fresh and hot." Kadicha-apa, the matriarch of the family refilled their bowls, making respectful hand motions as she did so. "How thin you are! It's clear that food was short on your long journey. Don't be shy! Eat up! You must replenish your strength to continue your journey."

"Thank you Kadicha-apa," answered Kanatbek. "It's been a long time since I was in this area and you probably don't remember me. I am Kanatbek, who served here alongside Tagay-bii. He and I arrived here exactly twelve years ago."

"Oh! Good heavens! Exclaimed Kadicha-apa. "Well I never… Now I remember! You and Tagay-bii left with your army to attend an important conference… How many years, how many winters have passed since then!

But I do remember you well! And your children – Dastan and Daniyar – how grown up they are! What a lot has happened since then. Sometimes, when my memory fails me, past events seem just like a dream…"

"And do you remember me, Kadicha-apa? I'm Saadat, Kanatbek's wife…"

"Gosh! Saadat! Of course I remember you! How glad we are that you've come back, Saadat! No-one could match the way you played the *dombra* [8] . Well, I'm honoured to have such guests! It's wonderful!"

The dinner was excellent and the travellers were more than appreciative of the lamb which they were sure would give them renewed strength and courage. After more stories and jokes, they were happy to retire to bed.

Kara-Choro however, slept fitfully. He felt overwhelmed with excitement about meeting his father and as soon as he fell asleep, he had vivid dreams about his beautiful mother Tomchi and how she would be worrying about him. He missed her and wondered when he would see her again. He also dreamt about his happy childhood and the village filled with people whom he loved and cared for. Everything which had been so comforting and familiar now seemed so far away.

Often, he woke up with a start in the middle of the night and leaving the yurt in search of fresh air, would sit on the ground gazing at the sky. The stars seemed so close that he imagined that he could reach up and touch them. When he lay back down to sleep, his dreams would then be filled with trepidation about the journey ahead to distant lands and the yet unknown experiences it would bring. At times, he wished that he could just run away from it all and scream and shout.

Unbeknown to poor Kara-Choro, such emotional turmoil was all part of the final step from childhood into manhood.

---

[7] *Elecheks is traditional head wear, worn by Kyrgyz women. It is made from light white cotton, rolled around the head and neck*

[8] *Dombra is Kazak musical instrument*

***

Next morning Kara-Choro, Kanatbek and their entourage left the yurt and set off on a walk along a little winding path. Soon they came to a place from which they could see a vast field full of red poppies. It was like a beautiful, bright carpet, which pleased the eye and raised everyone's spirits and in this region, many a young man had composed songs about the spectacular red poppies which to him, spoke of his eternal love for his beloved.

On that day however, it was the song of a young girl which touched their hearts. Accompanied by her *komuz* (Kyrgyz national musical instrument) , and wearing her hair in long plaits in hand, a teenage girl sang a beautiful and mournful song about a long, never-ending journey. The words and melody engrained themselves in Kara-Choro's soul, but he never suspected how prophetic the words of that song would be.

"Can dreams become reality?" Long and hard he gazed at the girl's face, listening to her voice… Later he found out that Nasipa – the name of the young fortune-teller – had composed her song almost instantly at the sight of the person to whom they were addressed and devoted.

"Dear boy, on your journey,
Think of your near ones and relatives;
Remember your destiny is not easy,
It draws you to distant lands;
I know you are ready to give
All the riches of the world
Only to see again one day
Those who you love as one family…"

As the girl sang, she watched Kara-Choro intently: her song was for him and him alone.

Kara-Choro and his companions went down to a spring, where they drank long of the cold, clean water. Refreshed and buoyed by the natural beauty around them, they returned to the yurt, where their hosts were waiting with a freshly prepared breakfast. Their hostess packed them a bag of food, and pointed out the quickest path to get to Kara-Choro's destination, the summer pastures of Tagay-bii.

Thanking and bidding their generous hosts goodbye, the travellers continued on their journey. As they ascended the steep and winding paths towards Song Kol, a breeze carried cool air down from the snowy peaks and they had to stop to put on extra layers of clothing. The tart smell of mountain herbs and the sharp cries of wild birds invigorated their spirits and soothed their souls. Up ahead, the Tien Shan Mountains rose to meet them, as majestic as the crown on a monarch's head.

"Kara-Choro, behind these mountains is China, the country from which silk, tea and other luxurious goods are carried through this valley." said Kanatbek. "Look, this is your homeland: The homeland of the Kyrgyz and your father, Tagay-bii!"

Suddenly a loud commanding voice stopped the travellers in their tracks.

"You there! Stop and dismount!" Two horsemen approached them, armoured warriors carrying bows, spears, and swords.

"Aidar! Don't you recognise us?" cried Kanatbek, looking closely at the approaching figures.

"Who are 'us'?"

"It's me, Kanatbek, with my wife Saadat and children!"

"Kanatbek, brother! Is it really you?" exclaimed one of the young soldiers in surprise and leaping from his horse, ran over to embrace Kanatbek.

"What a grown man you've become!" With tears of joy, Kanatbek took Aidar in his arms.

"Look who's here! It's Kanatbek himself!" Aidar turned to his companion, furtively wiping away a tear.

"Look at you now; a military leader! I remember teaching you how to shoot with a bow and defend yourself in combat. And now you're a man! How time flies!" Kanatbek held Aidar by the shoulders as he stood back from his friend, impressed by what had become of the boy he had mentored.

"Yes, that all seems so long ago now! And is this your son Dastan, the same playful mischief?" Aidar walked up to the horse, and helping the well-built, red-haired 25 year old dismount, gave him a tight hug. "How you have grown!"

"Assalaam aleikum, Aidar brother," greeted Dastan, joyfully.

"Oh, man! Valeikum assalaam!" Aidar answered the greeting with a firm manly handshake.

After everyone had exchanged greetings with Aidar and his companion, Kanatbek explained the reason for their visit: it was time to present Kara-Choro to his father.

"I hear and obey, Kanatbek, my brother!" said Aidar, and he ordered the second warrior to ride ahead and inform Tagay-bii himself about the arrival of Kara-Choro and the other guests.

***

When they arrived at the green pastures located beside the wondrous lake of Song Kol, Kara-Choro found it difficult to breathe, partly through anxiety and partly as a result of the thin mountain air and heady scent of the lush mountain pasture. In front of the largest yurt, which they approached accompanied by a warrior, Kara-Choro knelt down for a moment and kissed the grass. His eyes sparkled with excitement and his head was spinning. Now that the moment for which he had longed all his life had arrived, he suddenly felt physically detached from it all, as if he were watching the scene from above. Feeling light-headed, he nervously rehearsed in his mind yet again, what he should say when he met his father, and pulled out his father's pocket knife.

The door of the yurt was opened by a pretty, young girl who scowling, covered her face and ran off. And then, at last, it was time for Kara-Choro to meet his father.

"Assalaam Aleykum my northern Khan, Tagay-bii!" Kanatbek knelt and ordered his companions to do the same.

"O, valeykum assalaam, my friend Kanatbek!" Tall and imposing, with piercing green eyes, Tagay-bii stood up to greet the travellers.

"So, we've arrived, your excellency Tagay-bii!" said Kanatbek, hoarse with emotion.

"Welcome, my dear guests!" answered Tagay-bii in turn. Returning to his seat, he showed them the palms of his hands as a sign of respect and, with barely-controlled excitement, he continued watching them.

Kanatbek met Kara-Choro's glance and nodded, indicating that he should step forwards.

"Most esteemed northern Khan," began Kara-Choro. His throat was dry with anticipation: he had studied and memorised his speech so many times but now, at this long-awaited moment, found himself tongue-tied.

"I have news from you from my mother, Tomchi… My name is Kara-Choro… And this is your pocket knife, inscribed with your initials." The boy presented the Khan with his precious knife, still wrapped in its satin cloth.

Recognising his knife, Tagay-bii sighed and his eyes brightened and softened. He continued to hide his emotions, but his heart overflowed with happiness like burning lava: here, standing before him was his son!

"Let me have a closer look at it… Well, this certainly appears to be my knife," The northern Khan stared at Kara-Choro and then in a sudden burst of euphoria, jumped up and clutched his son to his chest, sobbing loudly with joy!

There wasn't a dry eye in the yurt as everyone silently watched the reunion of father and son.

Reluctant to free Kara-Choro from his tight embrace Tagay-bii continued to cry "My son, my son!"

Eventually, Tagay-bii released his son and asked them all to tell him about their journey.

Although Tagy-bii already knew Kanatbek's wife and family, Kara-Choro was becoming worried about whether the Khan would accept the other three boys in their group. Stepping forward, he decided to introduce them: "Father, these are my friends who joined us on the road. This is Bayisbek whom we met in Ichilik. He is studying how to use a bow and wants to join a caravan to go to Bukhara.

"My son, his name is no longer Bayisbek, but Sayak,[9] and he will also be a son to me," Tagay-bii replied firmly. "There is a saying, son. 'One man in a field is not a warrior.' Now he is my son and your brother!" And Tagay-bii clasped the boy who had escaped from the Dzungar massacre and was now named Sayak, to his chest.

"And this, with his large belly, is Azyk. During the trip he prepared our food," continued Kara-Choro, in a more confident and clear voice.

"Azyk, you will also be my son," responded Tagay-bii and with fatherly warmth, embraced to his son's second companion.

Turning to Kara-Choro's third companion, who stood quiet and wide-eyed at what was happening around him, the Khan then finished by stating: "You too, are also my son, and your name is Chertki."

Tagay-bii did not have it in his heart to expel any of the three strangers who had travelled so far with his blood son, Kara-Choro. Adopted as his children, they would grow to become his most loyal comrades. Tagay-bii was not only a fine politician, but also a man with a generous soul.

The Khan then ordered his servants to erect yurts for his new sons and let it be known that each one of them could choose himself a fine horse.

---

9 Sayak –foreigner , traveller, stranger (in Kyrgyz)

To celebrate the momentous occasion of the arrival of his son Kara-Choro and his new brothers from distant lands, Tagay-bii decided to host a great feast to which he would summon kin from all of the tribes.

***

Only one of Tagay-bii's circle was excluded, and for good reason. This was a man who at one time had betrayed his trust and insulted the merchants from Persia, who had often crossed these lands on route to Kashgar. The coarseness and ignorance displayed by this man had deeply undermined friendships and business relationships, built up over decades. The incident had occurred when Tagay-bii was at the conference hosted by the Bukhara Khan and the protagonist, Chap-Kene[10] , had not only unjustly insulted traders but had also attacked and robbed their caravan. For many years he had harboured a grudge against Tagay-bii's people and his dirty trick had benefited Tagay-bii's many enemies, since it had paved the way for similar acts of greed and selfishness. The story of the Persian merchants who had been insulted by Tagay-bii's thieving assistant drew unfavourable attention from all around the region and became a major cause of prejudice against Tagay-bii personally. It took him a great deal of time and effort to restore both the damaged trade relations and his reputation. The people depended on trade and the exchange of goods for their livelihood.

In his capacity as Tagay-bii's assistant, Chap-Kene had also, illegally, appropriated a lot of property and assets and in his own mind, at least, began to consider himself someone of high status within the community. Anyone who challenged his unfounded power was punished and when he discovered that Aidar, one of Tagay-bii's most loyal warriors, had questioned his actions, Chap-Kene immediately imprisoned him.

---

10 *Chap-Kene – a flea or louse. Someone who lives at the expense of others .Lazy, ignorant.*

In the Khan's absence, there was little hope of his being rescued but fortunately, Kadicha-apa, one of the eldest women in the village, was able to bring him food.

"Eat, Aidar," whispered Kadicha-apa, stealthily making her way to the dungeon at night. "You need strength; you can't live on empty pride. Conserve your strength. This won't continue for much longer. Last night, I dreamt that Tagay-bii is on his way home. Have patience. I don't know how many times I've warned Tagay-bii about Chap-Kene's schemes, but doting on him, he never took me seriously! 'Kadicha-apa' he told me. 'I know him like the back of my hand; he's still young and inexperienced but soon he'll become a man! No, before the Almighty and before Umay-ene, my conscience will be clear and I'll give him the chance to redeem himself".

Biting his lip with anger, Aidar heeded the advice of the wise old woman and bided his time, eating everything that was secretly brought to him. Kadicha-apa was right! He needed to keep his strength up. As the ancient eastern proverb decrees: "Live well today to fight tomorrow."

Tagay-bii's key concerns as a ruler were to maintain peace and prosperity for his country and he had committed his life, with fierce determination, to serving the clans who had elected and placed their trust in him. However, his experience as a political and military leader had taught him that there would always be those within his own community who driven by quests for personal gain and power, would challenge and threaten his authority and ultimately, strive to overthrow him.

On his return from Fergana, Tagay-bii was informed about his assistant's treachery and outraged by the severity of his actions, immediately renounced his friendship with Chap-Kene and banished both he and his wife from the region. Aidar, meanwhile, was released from the dungeon and as a reward for his loyal service to the community, promoted to the post of military commander.

"Just wait, Tagay-bii, I've not finished with you yet!" shouted Chap-

Kene as he and his furious were marched out of town.

"Be quiet! Keep calm and give nothing away! You must work out a strategy for your revenge. Give a sign to his enemies: tell them where he grazes his horse… May Tagay-bii be bitten by a poisonous snake, in the place he least expects!" Gritting her teeth in hatred of their former benefactor, his wife hissed instructions in his ear. Now she was dressed like a beggar.

"May God be with you, Chap-Kene," cried Kalicha-apa after them. "Although you have been shamed, repent of your mistakes! What happened to you? Didn't Tagay-bii trust you with his soul? How could you have abused such trust? And for what?! Everyone believed in you but you sold yourself to the Devil!"

***

As the years passed by, Kara Choro and his brothers became completely settled in their father's community, assisting him in all matters concerning clan unity and the development of Silk Route trade for the benefit of their people. They all married and had children, much to the delight of Tagay-bii who by then was growing old and beginning to lose his strength. One day, he called for his son Kara-Choro and with great reluctance and sadness announced:

"My son, my days are numbered and after I die, your life will be in great danger. The time has come for you to take leave of your brothers and run from here. My eldest wife's children will pursue and try to kill you, to prevent you from assuming power over the country after my death." Tagay-bii wiped his tears and handed Kara-Choro a handful of earth wrapped in a white cloth.

"This earth is Kyrgyz earth! The earth of your homeland! Take it Kara-Choro and when, at the end of your journey, far from here, you finally find a safe place to call your own, pour this soil into the ground and plant a tree. May it grow to be strong and healthy and always remind you of me!" and Tagay-bii held his son close.

"This is a sad day, father, but please don't worry!" Clutching the package to his breast, he comforted his father. "I give you my word that I will honour your request but must now go and tell my brothers about our plan."

***

Night fell and against the sounds of a light breeze rustling the leaves and the hunting cry of an owl, a whispered conversation could be heard from the yurt shared by Kara-Choro and his family. Sayak, Chertki and Azyk gazed sadly at their brother as he related their father's instructions, each man looking for the best way to save him.

"Well, Kara-Choro, we will stay here and fulfil our father's wish. We and our families will remain here and with the help of Umay-ene and Khan Tengri, we promise on our lives, to look after and protect your family as our own. We'll move to other pastures to ensure their safety. You, Kara-Choro, must now escape! We've already prepared two horses for you to accelerate your journey. If you leave before dawn, your enemies won't notice that you've gone until they wake up and you'll get a head start!" Sayak outlined their plan but little could console the brothers who realised that once Kara-Choro had left, they might never see each other again. Nobody knew what awaited Kara-Choro on his journey or what destiny he had in store.

After drinking kumys for courage and packing supplies of food, Kara-Choro galloped away before sunrise. Despite the need for haste, he could not leave the region before paying one last call to Nasipa, the young prophetess who had sung to him in Suusamyr, when he arrived to meet his father for the first time.

"Your song about my destiny was not meaningless and the day has come for me to leave your land, which has become my home. I don't know what awaits me in the future, Nasipa…"

"Do not despair, Kara-Choro! I have another prophecy for you. On your path, you will meet an elderly stranger. Invite him to continue his journey with you. In gratitude, the old man will help you in many ways, and will become like a father to you. He will lead you to the new land where you will realise your destiny and establish a new people. These people will hail from the mountains and their faith and traditions will be very like our own. Send me news of your progress through the caravans and I'll pass your wishes and news to your children and brothers. But now, you must get on your way Kara-Choro!" exclaimed the seer and lowering her eyes, pressed a silver coin into his hand for good luck.

"Onwards, my steed! Fly!" cried Kara-Choro. Looking back for one last time on Kyrgyz land, he crouched low on his horse and waved his whip.

"Preserve this man, O great Khan Tengri! Teach him the way of Truth and lead him to his cherished goal!" prayed Nasipa after him.

As he rode further and further away from the land of his father and from the family which he loved, this final encounter remained ingrained in Kara-Choro's memory for a very long time and was a source great strength, hope and comfort as he entered foreign territories.

People from the caravans spoke of how they had seen Kara-Choro on the road to the Caucasus accompanied by an old man and years later, as predicted by the almond eye Nasipa, Kara-Choro did indeed establish his own khanate with the Karachay people.

And so ended this part of J.M's richly woven story about the union between Tagay-bii and Tomchi, the power of predestination and how its impact upon the life and trade of the ancients created a well of wisdom which continues to influence contemporary life.

***

... Doctor Brandon Silver listened to J.M's story in awe and when she had finished, he removed his horn-rimmed glasses and sat for a long time, wiping his tears. Her boss's emotional reaction to her narrative was an unexpected and pleasant surprise for J.M.

From the street they heard voices, signalling the end of daytime activity and the start of the Edinburgh's night life when the city's streets, pends and alleyways were filled with people either making their way home from work or emerging to explore the city's nooks and crannies as they made their way to pubs, clubs and restaurants. Immune to the lure of the city's attractions and too absorbed in their work to leave, the two indefatigable researchers remained in their office.

A nip of whisky, imbued with the aroma of fresh honey and a delicate infusion of oak, warmed and cheered them as they worked on, oblivious to both the atrocious weather and everything that was going on outside.

"Doctor Silver is anything the matter?" asked J.M. languorously, still immersed in the vision of her narrative. She touched her boss's shoulder to rouse him from his deep thoughts.

"Huh? What?" asked Dr Silver, rising and topping up his glass of Glenmorangie with water, whilst adjusting his spectacles.

"I've been a historian for many years, but this is the first time that I've felt so entranced by such a colourful account of ancient events. It's as though I were actually there!

Why haven't you told me this before?" Dr Silver continued, finishing his whisky.

"Dear Miss J.M., after we finish what we are doing tomorrow you must continue the story. After all, you haven't told me all of it yet, have you?" Dr Silver looked at his assistant with eyes shining and a curious smile.

"With pleasure, Dr Silver," responded J.M. They called a taxi, closed the huge doors of the building and set the alarm. As they were locking up, she had felt an urge to tell her boss about the cloaked stranger in the unusual cloak whom she had seen lurking in the shadows the previous night but since it was already late and she could see nothing untoward this evening, she dismissed the idea and bade him goodnight.

Returning home, she found that a letter had arrived from the antiquarian which she assumed to contain archival material concerning her silver lamp. Inside the envelope, which had a strange return address, she found a single sheet of paper on which text had been written in an incomprehensible text. After searching the internet she eventually discovered that the text had been written in Nordic runes and after another hour spent with an online translator it transpired that the lamp had been brought into Britain by Scandinavian settlers who had settled here in the mid sixteenth century. The document held no further information of any relevance. Slightly disappointed, though not discouraged, she decided to pay a repeat visit to the kind, merry-eyed antiques dealer.

That night, J.M. had a dream: The same dream she had had many times as a child…

In it, she found herself beside the long and winding river where she had often walked with neighbours' children to collect water during her school holidays. There she was, J.M. as a little girl, staring into the river as she dipped her bucket. Her eye is caught by something sparkling in the water among the pebbles. Looking closely, she sees the reflection of a young girl wearing a gold medallion around her neck. This sad and strikingly amazingly beautiful girl has secrets that she needs to share. She beckons to J.M. to come closer so that she can whisper something in her ear. J.M. leans forwards until strands of her hair float on the surface but suddenly, the water ripples lightly and the image of the girl disappears in a flash of light. All that is left on the river bed are pebbles and weeds. Frustrated, J.M. stands up and steps away from the river but as she does so, feels something weighing heavily around her thin neck and putting her hand up, discovers that she is now wearing the other girl's gold medallion!

J.M.'s delight at this discovery is so intense, so believable, that she immediately awakes and automatically touches her neck and chest in search of this wonderful gift…

Year after year, she has experienced this exact same dream, and even after waking tonight, she feels a great sense of loss and disappointment when she discovers that the medallion is missing!

***

The next morning, J.M. immediately returned to the area of the city where she had found the shop. It was her intention to firstly thank the dealer for the curious information he had provided, and to then try to procure from him any further information, no matter how scant, that he might have about her lamp. In addition, since she was certain that she had seen him somewhere before, she was keen to try to clarify where and when that might have been; over the cup of coffee he had promised her. In her capacity as an experienced and sensitive researcher, she was well versed in gaining people's confidence when requiring them to provide her with information.

The door of the antique shop was locked and when she rang the bell, she was surprised when it was opened by a young woman wearing a modern, asymmetric hairstyle, and wire-rimmed glasses perched on the tip of her small pointed nose. She in turn, was puzzled to hear that J.M. wanted to talk to the "elderly, dark-skinned and grey-eyed" owner since she had never come across anyone matching that description in this shop. J.M's detailed descriptions of the silver lamp, and how and when she had purchased it, were also met with blank stares. The assistant began to lose her patience when J.M. presented her with the letter, insisting that since the shop had never stocked such a lamp and consequently, had no record of such in either their stock sheets or archives. Nor had they ever received enquiries about a lamp of this description from any of their clients.

In utter confusion, J.M. mumbled her thanks to the saleswoman and apologised for any inconvenience caused. She left the shop and walked, deep in thought, down a steep flight of stairs which would take back her to the main thoroughfare. She couldn't work out what had happened to the antiques dealer who had apparently disappeared. And who were those other two people, the by standing customers who had been so delighted that she had bought the lamp, and even happier that they had persuaded her to barter for it! Why on earth would the shop assistant whom she had met this morning, categorically deny that the purchase of the lamp had even taken place or that any correspondence about its provenance had been sent from the shop? There was no doubt in J.M's mind that she had visited the correct shop, so what was going on? Even if her recollection of the appearances of the three people had been affected in some way by the notion that she had met them before, she still had the lamp, so the entire episode had definitely not been a figment of her imagination…

It suddenly dawned on J.M. that, of course, the images which she held in her mind of these mysterious people corresponded exactly with those of characters described by her grandfather Toktogul's tale about Kara-Choro. They had dwelt in her mind for many years and now she recognised that the physical appearance of the dealer matched that of the old man who met Kara-Choro on his journey and continued with him to the new land! But who did the other two customers remind her of?

Chapter VII

The White Knights of the Peterson Clan

The fog covered the city so thickly that houses and trees seemed to disappear within an arm's length and only the light from street lamps, traffic lights and car headlights broke through the dense blue haze. For anyone with a fairly vivid imagination, which undoubtedly applied to J.M., this meteorological phenomenon ,common in these parts , seemed supernatural; an allegorical confrontation between the forces of darkness and light. From the window of her cosy apartment, J.M. could watch a kind of three-dimensional shadow theatre focusing on the centuries-old struggle of the city against the ravages of time, filled with the pathos of the everyday lives of its inhabitants.

After a while, she carefully set down her cup of unfinished, hot tea, closed the curtains and stepped deeper into the room. Opening a safe built into the wall, she picked up the silver lamp which she had purchased the day before and placed it inside next to a very old catalogue in a brown leather cover. For some time she looked at both objects with a smile on her face, one hand stroking the fine geometric patterns on the lamp, and the other hand caressing the rough embossing on the book cover. Then she frowned and looked around anxiously. The feeling that she was constantly being watched had stayed with her for a second day. J.M. carefully closed the safe and hid the key under the felt doll dressed in the Kyrgyz traditional costume of a married woman, embroidered with a Tien Shan trefoil: a gift brought from her family home many years ago.

Finishing her tea, she checked her mobile phone. She had missed several calls. Her heart skipped a beat: all the calls were from Dr Silver. They had been made during the night and in the early morning.

J.M. quickly got ready and left for the Centre. Greeting Mrs Jane

McKendry, she explained that she would have to entertain the guests at the Centre before joining Dr Silver, who had been delayed at the dentist and would be late. She did not know the real reason for his absence.

Many delegates had already arrived and were eagerly waiting for the meeting to begin. Stepping up to the podium and switching on the microphone, J.M. welcomed everyone and apologised for Dr Silver's delayed appearance which were "due to circumstances beyond his control."

The guests continued talking with each other, looking at the items and documents exhibited in one of the Centre's halls. Mrs Jane McKendry informed the curious guests about how the LMR Centre had evolved, the deplorable state of the building prior to the appointment of Dr Silver and his associates, and about the unfortunate fate of the original building, which had been virtually destroyed by a terrible fire. J.M. could not help noticing Mrs McKendry's dreamy, nostalgic smile when she spoke of the "terrible fire". But, continued the old woman, waving her arms pathetically, the cunning intruders were powerless in the face of Providence, and they did not succeed in completely destroying this magnificent example of 17th century Scottish Gothic architecture. For many years neither the Edinburgh municipal authorities nor private charitable organisations had the courage or resources to reconstruct the building. And the first attempt to restore the premises and then use it to house the LMR Historical Analytical Centre was only made in 2001.

"Oh yes, what a lot of effort they put into it!" continued Miss Jane McKendry, with dry lips primly pursed, and many in the audience thought they heard a touch of schadenfraude in her voice. "Throughout the building there was a smell of ash and foul water, the stench of local drunks and drug addicts who took shelter here: dirt and dust everywhere. Huge rats scurried across the roof and floors, making an odious sound with their small claws, like the clattering of a hundred typewriters. Heaps of dried pigeon droppings up to half a metre high… All of this created such an unbearable smell that it could only be averted with special masks…" continued Mrs McKendry in a loud and sing-song voice.

Dr Silver arrived at last and interrupting the old woman announced: "Ladies and gentleman, a thousand apologies for the delay! Good morning everyone, and to you too, my dear Mrs McKendry. Unfortunately, unexpected circumstances held me up this morning but now that I'm here, let's get to work…"

His presentation proved a great success and there were many questions afterwards: clearly the life and character of the young and eminent nobleman Learmonth, the ancestor of Russian writer Lermontov, had captivated the audience.

***

"Gosh, what an interesting and stressful day," said Dr Silver, sighing deeply. He made himself a strong coffee, then sat down in his favourite chair and began to explain why he had been late.

"Today, a very good friend of mine is supposed to be flying in from Iceland," he said, looking mischievously at his assistant.

"Which good friend?" asked J.M., pouring herself a tea and looking suspiciously at Dr Silver?

"The representative of the very same Peterson Clan that you heard about before," replied Dr Silver, smiling enigmatically and savouring his strong coffee.

"Well, that would be nice and useful to all of us, especially since you've wanted to invite your friend to our Centre for ages. As I recall, your main reason for having him visit was to allow him direct insight into what the office does and to introduce him to the history and attractions of the city, particularly those places where the great scholar Adam Smith lived and worked." Smiling sweetly, J.M. finished typing on her laptop, pulled the records out of her bag, and settled comfortably with her tea in her hand. She was about to continue yesterday's story when suddenly there was a knock on the Centre's front door.

"Who's there?" called out Dr Silver in surprise, as he rose and began walking along the dark corridor to the entrance.

"It's the Post!" Dr Silver opened the door and let in a blonde man of average height with a bit of a belly. His accent suggested that he was originally from Poland. In his hands he held a medium-sized parcel.

After seeing him out, Dr Silver with childlike excitement began to open the carefully-packed box. He pulled out a slender and beautiful bottle, and a glass jar labelled "Dried Shark Meat".

"As always, my friend has been very attentive. Before every visit, he sends such delicacies: an allusion to the fact that here in Scotland we cannot buy any Icelandic spirits or dried shark meat!" Smiling contentedly, Dr Silver offered J.M. a taste.

The young woman refused, expressly pursing her lips and shaking her head. Then she smiled politely and began recalling at what point she had halted her epic narrative last time.

All of a sudden, strange noises were heard from outside. They were unsure if it was the howling of the wind or people squabbling but either way, it made J.M. and Dr Silver very uneasy.

"Does it seem to you that we're not alone?" Dr Silver stood up anxiously and locked the safe containing the Centre's most important documents.

The very next moment the power failed, something that had not happened at the Centre for a long time, plunging the building into darkness.

"Stay with me," whispered Dr Silver, pulling out a small torch that was attached to the chain of keys that he carried in his trouser pocket.

"What the hell?" exclaimed J.M. as she suddenly caught sight of a group of masked figures in the dim corridor, led by someone wearing a black coat and mask and wielding an old revolver.

"Aha! What are you two up to now: scheming behind my back again?" tutting and shaking his head, the leader removed the mask and was revealed to be none other than Jane McKendry. Turning to the two stalwart companions, she motioned to them to tie up Dr Silver and his assistant.

"What on earth do you think you are doing, Mrs Jane McKendry?" Dr Silver spoke first, recovering from his surprise.

"Ha – you don't need to call me that any longer," answered the caretaker, smiling maliciously and putting down the old revolver, decorated with little toothed and tailed devils.

"Did you honestly think that you could carry on with all of this, without us, the Blackdales Clan? You obviously decided against sharing any of the secrets or treasure that you've discovered over the past few days and you really believed that we were incapable of overhearing your conversations and hence, oblivious to your plans." Squeezing together her thin lips, painted with bright-pink lipstick, the woman took off her gloves, sat down on the chair recently vacated by Dr Silver, and gave orders to her accomplices to take his keys and search both the room and J.M.'s bag and personal belongings.

"So this gang of thugs has been watching my assistant and I all this time," thought Dr Silver. He indignantly addressed their leader:

"You don't know what to do with this lamp in any case!"

"And what do you think we need you for, dearie? You think it's just you that's so smart, eh?" Walking closer to Dr Silver and pointing the gun at JM, she ordered the doctor to show her the place in the port registration document where only yesterday, they had found something of particular significance.

Not finding anything in the room, the assistants of the woman who called herself Jane McKendry stood at either side of their boss.

"Tell me where you've hidden the silver lamp!" shouted the quavering voice of the Blackdales' leader, now pushing the muzzle of gun against Dr

Silver.

"Wait! The silver lamp is at my home, in the safe! Please don't shoot! We can all go over to my place and I'll get it for you! Terrified, J.M. hastily intervened.

"Don't tell these fools anything: you still don't know the purpose of the lamp, or the significance of the story behind it! They just want to spit over our academic work." barked Dr Silver.

One of the masked men hit him across his temple and Dr Silver passed out as he fell to his knees.

"Shut up, you bald idiot! Look how agitated he is!" the Blackdales' clan leader shouted. "What makes you think we don't know what to do with the treasure? Right: go to the car! Load the baldie in the boot," she ordered her assistants with a grin.

***

Dr Silver was still unconscious when the two masked men dragged him out and loaded him into the boot of the car. J.M., with her hands tied, was taken to her flat, and the bandits removed the silver lamp from the safe. Then, covering her head with a bag, they drove both of the unfortunate researchers far from the city.

Dr Silver and J.M. were dumped in a cave which by chance, contained a famous labyrinth which had been well documented. This cave had served as an exit point to the sea and in the past, missionaries had hidden here from their enemies, before making their way through the long maze to the shore of the North Sea, and thence to a merchant ship bound for another country.

When he regained consciousness, Dr Silver found himself lying next to J.M. with his hands tied behind his back.

"Are you all right, Miss J.M.?" he asked, clearing his throat and turning to his assistant. He was happy to find that miraculously, she had somehow managed to free herself from the ropes which had bound her.

"Don't worry about me: I'm quite all right," smiled J.M. encouragingly, whilst putting her finger to her lips to indicate that he should talk quietly. She immediately began to untie his hands.

"How could I have let such a thing happen?" lamented Dr Silver, shaking his head. He was still in a state of shock because he had failed to recognise the dastardly plans of the evil old woman, whom he had always known as Mrs Jane McKendry.

Although no longer tied up, they continued to sit closely side by side, with their arms positioned as if still bound, so as not to arouse suspicion from the masked guards.

"I need to think this through carefully," whispered Dr Silver, and picking up a stick that lay nearby, he began to draw a plan of the maze from memories of descriptions found in textbooks.

"We need to determine from which side we entered this labyrinth, as it contains many dead ends that would prevent our escape. What vultures they are: they've even taken my pocket torch!" growled Dr Silver angrily.

"Luckily, I still have a torch: I always carry it with me just in case." J.M. tried to calm her boss and checking that the guards were elsewhere, extracted a small torch from her pocket and directed its beam on the rough map drawn by Dr Silver.

"And what possessed you to give them the silver lamp?" asked Dr Silver, ruefully.

"They don't know what to do with it. At least I now know that Daria was here and left a record. That was the sign that I have been seeking for so long. Those scoundrels won't glean anything from that inscription, which in any case, I've copied. They have no inkling about the essence of the story: I alone, know its secrets!" comforted J.M., with a charming smile.

Having worked out their route through the labyrinth, they then waited for dusk to fall, so that they could escape under the cover of darkness.

"What are you whispering about?" asked one of the masked men, coming over to them. "Just sit still and shut up!" As soon as his back was turned, J.M. stealthily handed Dr Silver a Taser gun which she had ingeniously managed to secrete from her safe and hide in her clothes. Wasting no time, Dr Silver immediately sprang to his feet and aimed the gun at the neck of the guard who had just turned to leave. As he pressed the button, Dr Silver watched with pleasure as the man was knocked unconscious. Removing his mask, they gasped in amazement as they recognised the postman with a Polish accent!

For a while they looked at him dumbfounded, and then they looked at each other. After firmly tying him up and blasting him another precautionary, electric shock, they set off to find their way out of the maze.

***

They ran for a long time, sometimes stumbling upon dead ends, before eventually finding the exit in the early morning. Never had they been so bewitched by the sunrise over the North Sea!

"Fresh air, at last!" exclaimed J.M. in a pitched voice. The escapees, tired, dirty and hungry, stopped to catch their breath.

"Who would have dreamt that we would have been caught up in something like this!" lamented Dr Silver.

"I'm just so relieved that we're out of there!" Taking a deep breath, J.M. supported her boss and began to brush down his clothes.

"On the day, when we were looking through old records, I had a feeling that someone was watching me. It's difficult to explain: the candle we had lit at the Centre entrance was flickering as if unsettled by movement and I thought I caught a glimpse of a man lurking in the shadows. I should have voiced my suspicions but we were so engrossed by the silver lamp, that I completely forgot. Who would have thought that it would lead to this?" concluded J.M., removing her shoes and shaking out the sand.

"So, what are our plans? This old witch, the leader of the Blackdales vultures, is turning our Centre inside out , in search of something that she thinks will reveal your secret, even though she has no idea what that might be. That means we have enough time to get in touch with my friend from the Peterson Clan since it's possible that he's already arrived. I'm just afraid however, that they'll catch him, just as they caught us... What can we do? We can't even call him since both of our phones are dead!" he exclaimed in frustration, scratching his bald head.

"Dr Silver, look: there's a little house over there. Perhaps we can use their phone to contact the police?" J.M. pointed to a wooden fishing hut about half a mile away. Without hesitation they set off along the shore towards the house.

***

To their utter astonishment, the man who opened the door of the hut was none other than Dr Silver's friend, John Peterson!

"Well, here we all are, together at last! I've been waiting for you, Dr Silver!" Peterson looked bemused as shook the hand of his old and dear friend. The Icelander was tall with brown hair and swiftly appraised by J.M, was met with an approving glance which he was not slow to return.

"What on earth are you doing here?" Still recovering from his amazement, Dr Silver smiled happily as he looked in admiration at his colleague. "But anyway... I'd like you to meet Miss J.M., my assistant. I've told you a lot about her and her stories over the phone..."

"I'm delighted to meet you! My name is John Peterson." Captivated by her beauty, he held her cold hands in his for some time and found himself unable to tear his gaze from her.

as they silently looked at one another. J.M. smiled shyly and did not understand what was happening to her…

"As soon as I pulled up to your Centre," explained John Peterson, guiding them into the house and pulling up a chair at a small wooden table, "I witnessed three masked men making a hasty getaway and was even more surprised when I saw them loading you, Dr Silver, into the boot of their car!" Laughing, he looked towards Dr Silver, who reddening at this reminder of the undignified manner in which he had been treated, gasped: "So you didn't leave the taxi but rushed after us? Thank God, you arrived when you did!"

The Icelander prepared some hot coffee and served them sandwiches which he had had the foresight to pick up on his journey from the airport to the city. He had suspected that something had gone terribly wrong when he had been unable to reach them by phone.

"When you called me two days ago, you asked me to come over because you wanted to share some extraordinary discoveries which you had made. You also revealed your suspicions that a faction of the Blackdales Clan was still active. At the time I was doubtful, because I was certain that the Clan had been completely neutralised by my Clan 200 years ago." As he spoke, John Peterson's pale blue eyes would soften whenever they fell upon J.M.

"So what made you change your mind?" Dr Silver was engrossed.

"I came to Scotland out of curiosity but everything that happened last night has more than convinced me that your suspicions were correct. I watched them take Miss J.M with her hands tied, into her flat in Bruntsfield and then followed their car with both of you inside, to the cave. Afterwards, I drove to your Centre where I found this old book with a page torn out. I then called the police, to report the kidnapping and to request that they guard the Centre against further theft and the removal of any evidence of both your capture and the robbery. Meanwhile, contacts whom I had alerted at the time of the kidnapping had continued to follow the Blackdales' car after it left the cave and as a result, I can now tell you exactly where the scoundrels are hiding!" John Peterson finished his account and took a sip of his freshly-brewed coffee.

"So what happens next? Our main concern is that those villains now have the silver lamp along with the documentation, which they naively believe they will be able to decipher without us," noted Dr Silver unhappily.

"Don't worry, doctor, I beg you! I can assure you that under no circumstances, will they succeed in revealing the secrets held by the lamp!" Suddenly overcome with fatigue, J.M. excused herself and went outside to breathe in the fresh sea air. Everything had happened so fast and although she knew that the stolen material would prove useless to the Blackdales, she was terrified that she would never recover the objects which offered critical, long sought and tangible support for her research thesis.

Inside, John Peterson received a call on his mobile phone.

"Hello, this is John… Yes, hello Steven," replied Peterson. Heading outside, he was happy to have a chance to have a closer view of J.M' shapely figure as she stood with her back towards him, deep in thought.

"That's fantastic! We're at the fisherman's hut near the cave of the maze. See you soon, my friend!" Peterson finished the conversation and went down to the shore to join J.M.

"Great news, Miss J.M! One of my colleagues has found your mobile phone and your handbag. You mentioned earlier that they contained important records, so now you'll now be able to show me how you were able to unravel so many mysteries, yes?" Smiling politely, John Peterson fixed his eyes on J.M.

In their absence, Dr Silver had been rooting about in the basement of the fisherman's hut and he was now yelling to them in great excitement: "Come here: Quickly!"

"What is it, doctor, have you found something?" J.M. and Peterson immediately ran to the hut.

"Yes, yes! Have a look at this! It's part of an old map which I found, well preserved, amongst the rubble in the basement!" Doctor Silver held out a piece of yellowed parchment on which were displayed several signs, numbers and directions.

Their inspection was momentarily halted by the arrival of a group of powerfully-built, young men, whom John introduced as his brothers in the Peterson Clan; a secret society that had been waging war against the cruel Blackdales Clan for centuries.

"John, here is the handbag we found discarded by the gate of Miss J.M.'s place. It clearly didn't contain anything of any use to them! The rest of our guys are now following the trail of the Blackdales' matriarch, who is better known in the city by the name Jane McKendry," explained Steven Peterson quickly. He then led John Peterson, Dr Silver and his assistant to his car and drove them into the city where accompanied by a police escort, they continued to the Centre on Lauriston Road.

Having already examined the old building, a police inspector questioned all three about what had happened the day before. Once satisfied that the Centre's staff was no longer at risk, the police departed, promising to inform them immediately if Mrs Jane McKendry was found.

"Finally we're alone!" smiled Dr Silver wearily, summing up a long day. He now prepared to uncork a dusty bottle of a very rare whisky found by the police in Mrs Jane McKendry's secret safe, but fortunately, not seized as evidence.

"Well, Miss J.M., please tell us everything you know, down to the last detail! John and I will listen to you carefully." Dr Silver invited his guest from Iceland to make himself comfortable, gave him a glass of whisky and then settled himself down with his own glass, in a rocking chair by the window.

Glancing at her audience, Miss J.M. continued her tale.

"This part of the story happened in the second half of the sixteenth century," began J.M., looking thoughtfully at the two men sitting near her, and tugging at the end of the Scottish plaid draped over her shoulders. "That was the time when the Golden Horde had already weakened and lost its influence in Eurasia. Many Tatar princes passed into the service of Muscovy (Moscow). There were radical changes in the political and economic life of the region. A new era began in Russia, the echoes of which were heard until the dawn of modern humanity, and indeed, to this very day.

The young woman kept looking towards Dr Silver and John Peterson but her inner gaze, pierced through the veil of centuries, was now sweeping through the drenched golden birch groves of another world, another era. Thus transported, J.M was no longer connected to the present: she had no idea what year it was; she only knew was that it was autumn…

Chapter VIII

Eshen-Kareg and his three sons

For a third successive day, warm September air caressed the travellers, who were making their way from Kazan to Moscow moving at the invitation of the Russian Tsar, Ivan the Terrible. They would then continue onwards to Alexander's Settlement,   where people, in the service of the State, were toiling day and night, to establish a grand administrative centre for Rus.

***

Alexander Settlement: From December 1564 to 1581, this was Ivan the Terrible's administrative capital. It was surrounded by dense forests, monasteries and fortresses. Foreign ships sailed here, carrying goods from England, Denmark and other countries. Two thirds of Russia' trade turnover with foreign countries passed through the Settlement. It housed papermaking, and a printing area which published religious and other books, including promotional materials, including some for foreign countries. There were also foreign embassies and ambassadors were received here...

In the Settlement state officials oversaw new reforms, copied chronicles of the country's history and establishing connection with Roman Emperors...

The state library was established hundreds of years before Ivan the Terrible. It began to be actively replenished following the beginning of the persecution of pagans. Books were confiscated from disgraced princes, nobles, merchants, and monasteries, as well as from incorporated and conquered peoples from Great Perm, Great Tyumen, the Volga, the Urals, Siberia and so on...

The peoples of our country had many books and libraries. A significant proportion were written and copied by bards (*akyns*), priests and educators…

Books were also imported from abroad (from China to England) in noisy fairs, where they were bought, exchanged and translated.

***

Their journey took them through a landscape of seemingly endless meadows, punctuated by lakes and rivers and flanked by forests. At regular intervals, they came across farmers' wooden houses surrounded by neat stacks of freshly cut hay. Epic Russ was revealed before them in all its glory but heeding the shortening hours and the chill winds, they could not afford to linger. All of Nature's verdant splendour now bathed by the late autumn sunshine would soon disappear under deep, white snowdrifts.

The most senior member of this group of nobles from Kazan, distinguished by his white beard and high forehead, was a man named Eshen-Kareg .

Kareg: the highest academic degree of the Tatar nobility, with the status of academic.

Prior to the collapse of the Golden Horde, he had held a high position in the Court of Kazan and the Khan had bestowed upon him the honour of "Kareg" in recognition of his services.

He was indebted to his ancestors for his scholastic career, position in Court and significant wealth, but it was on account of his own academic achievements that Eshen-Kareg had been invited by Ivan the Terrible, the first Tsar of Muscovy, to assist in drawing up a draft for the Tsarevo Liberia.

***

Liberia: the famous (*hypothetical*) library of Ivan the Terrible, where he kept rare manuscripts, parchments, Latin chronicles ancient Egyptian manuscripts, labels and textbooks from the Mongol khans, and books of the East and other peoples. The underground vaults and recesses also contained ancient Slavic, Scythian and other nations' chronicles, as well as the richest collections of books imported from Novgorod, Tver, Vladimir, Suzdal, Pskov ...

***

It was a great honour for Eshen-Kareg and the Great Tsar had chosen wisely since the realisation of the Liberia required great knowledge, creative strength and a flawless work ethic. The Library was a treasure trove of human culture, the greatness of which not even the Tsar completely understood.

After a long day on the road, the travellers decided to stop for the night and set up camp in a meadow between an ancient, dense forest and a river. Eshen-Kareg's three sons, Ibragim, Sadyk and Yusuf, shot some ducks and collected berries and mushrooms for dinner and then exhausted, everyone retired to bed.

Eshen-Kareg's youngest son, Yusuf, had a dream that night which he never remembered. All that remained was a strange premonition of impending disaster, which haunted him over the days that followed. He couldn't qualify his reasons for feeling so anxious especially since their highly esteemed father had been summoned by the Tsar himself to lead such an important project.

Yusuf was awoken by the neighing and thundering sound of horses' hooves as the royal carriage sped past their tents. The carriage was protected by many mounted Tsarist soldiers wearing long-skirted kaftans of red cloth. The gold buttons on their coats and their curved sabres glinted in the sun, causing Yusuf to squint as he watched them pass.

"Yusuf, cover yourself up or you'll catch a cold," called Eshen-Kareg, returning with water from the river. "It looks as though we're not far away from the town of Moscow."

"Look, Yusuf," continued Eshen-Kareg enthusiastically. "Rest your eyes on this wonderful landscape which Nature has filled with such indescribable beauty! Russia! Great and fair Russia! Soon the dreary rain will commence and these wonderful hues will fade to grey. And all that will remain will be bare trees, black shapes against the white snow, waiting stoically for next spring… Pack your things and harness the horses: it's time to move on." He roused the others and then helped Yusuf saddle his horse.

Ibragim and Sadyk, Yusuf's elder brothers, watched this scene with annoyed smirks, wondering what it was about Yusuf that made their father indulge him so. Granted, Yusuf was naturally highly intelligent, and had shown a flair for languages from an early age. He could talk for hours with his father about distant lands, their people and their habits, always hoping to travel the world with him one day. But what use was such enthusiasm for philosophical talk and debate in the practical world? Pushing aside their grudges, and keen to get going, they obediently followed their father's command and quickly mounted their horses. Soon the whole group was on its way again towards Moscow.

***

Times were hard. Shortly before these events, when the Golden Horde was still intact and before Ivan the Terrible came to power, ancient Russia was in a lamentable state, subject to endless invasions and wars. The poverty of its people was visible everywhere.

In view of all these problems, the Tsar was determined to change Rus. In less than no time Moscow town was transformed into a centre of culture.

Not far from Moscow, surrounded by wild forests and newly constructed monasteries and fortresses, an administrative centre was established in the urban settlement of Alexandrov. This was where all of the printing presses were located, decrees were issued and many historical books were copied.

Yusuf observed all of these developments with great pleasure, and was happy to help his father and his entourage with the extensive and arduous task of creating the Library of Ivan the Terrible, the first Tsar of Muscovy.

Ivan the Terrible was only three years old when illness killed his father and so he was forced to grow up without any parental guidance or protection against the political wrangling and battles for individual power which were rife in the imperial palace and often led to bloodshed. Acts of cruelty and treachery fuelled by suspicion, ambition and deception were commonplace and provided the young man with a model which would adversely influence his style of government.

By the time he came to power, Ivan the Terrible possessed an extraordinary and subtle intellect but was also imperious and irascible, selfish and cruel, and was renowned for tormenting his subjects and instilling wide-spread fear. His restless temperament also drove him to amass many concubines and mistresses, whilst retaining several wives, each bound to fulfil his whims and gratify his lust.

According to legends, by the time the Tsar had turned thirteen, he had already lived a wild and debauched life, and slept with many girls. As a consequence, he fathered numerous illegitimate children, who had to remain hidden for their own protection against the evil eye as well as the Tsar's wives and legitimate children. The latter had a hard time too. During his lifetime, the first Tsar of Muscovy married eight times. As a rule, very few of either his wives and or his children lived to old age since the brutal treatment to which they were subjected by the hands of bitterly jealous, senior wives, often proved fatal. And no-one was exempt from the wrath of the Tsar, who was known to have ordered one of his first wives to be harnessed to horses and deposited in a pond where she was left to drown and be eaten by the fish.

The Tsar's eyes burned like dark amber and it was believed that the spirit of the devil himself sat within him, manipulating his violent mood swings. Yet paradoxically, his thirst for knowledge, passion for reading, and frequent displays of eloquence amazed and enthralled both his entourage and ordinary Russian people from all walks of life. It was said that the Library created by Tsar Ivan the Terrible served as his only escape from the poisonous atmosphere of slander, intrigue and backbiting, and that by reading and rereading his books, the Tsar found rare moments of peace and personal happiness.

***

Many of the chroniclers who worked to create the Library suffered from the poor working conditions and in particular, from the spores produced by mould growing on the damp underground walls. The rooms and passages were cramped and poorly lit by candles and burners fuelled by animal fat which emitted thick and pungent smoke. Literally hundreds of workers were employed in the mammoth task of transcribing and cataloguing archival records and republishing books by printing scripts on the heavy presses, and anyone descending the stairs from the halls of the main library felt that they were entering another, hidden world filled with the whirring of large machines and scratching quills.   Working in such conditions took its toll on the workers' eyesight, backs and lungs and there was no relief at night when they were expected to sleep on bunks roughly constructed from planks of wood. Despite all, the workers did enjoy a level of camaraderie and in the evenings, over bottles of English port provided by the Court, they would entertain each other with stories of their homelands and loved ones, poetry, music, song and of course political debate.

The Tsar had decreed that days off could be taken on Sundays and whenever their turn came to escape from the gloom of the cellars, everyone fled the Alexander settlement to enjoy the fresh air of the countryside or the bright lights Moscow and the town's markets, fairs and cultural attractions. They could also attend ceremonial parades and games or witness executions which were scheduled in accordance with the Tsar's volatile mood.

Eshen-Kareg and his three sons naturally looked forward to these holidays when they could enjoy being outside and discovering more about Russian traditions and customs. On one of their Sunday trips from Alexander Settlement to Moscow, Yusuf was passed on the road by the Tsar's guard who were accompanying a coach. Through a small gap in the coach's dark curtains, Yusuf glimpsed a young girl and was immediately entranced by the sight of her large, blue eyes which framed by long dark lashes were filled with sorrow and suffering. Yusuf stopped in his tracks as if struck by lightning.

He later found out that the girl was Ivan the Terrible's illegitimate daughter, who was being watched by guards day and night, prior to her being sent abroad to wed. Such marriages typically served as guarantees for the development of trade and economic ties between Russia and Europe.

No one knew or had heard which foreign country she was destined for, or where her betrothed was from. This was a strictly guarded secret and anyone who spoke of it would be sent to the gallows by imperial decree.

At that moment however, as Yusuf stood rooted to the spot oblivious to her identity, he experienced a strange sense of predestination which sharply echoed the feeling of supressed terror he had felt when waking from his dream on his family's journey to Moscow.

Seeing his son's pale demeanour, Eshen-Kareg asked anxiously:

"My son, what's wrong? Are you unwell? Perhaps you've contracted a fever from the damp conditions in the library basement?"

"Don't worry, Father, it's not that. I've wanted to tell you something for a long time: I've been haunted by thoughts and dreams that I don't understand... My inner voice tells me that we must be cautious."

"It'll be alright, Yusuf. Don't worry. If you can't cope with your anxiety, I will talk with the Chamber and see if they can transfer you to a good position in Moscow. You could teach the nobles' children there because you have a talent for it! You were an excellent student and– your skills should be acknowledged."

"Oh Father, we don't need to do anything so drastic! It's not the damp, but some feeling continues to haunt me... I don't know what it is: I'm very confused..."

"Perhaps you're just ill, my son." Eshen-Kareg put his hand to his son's forehead and commanded that they get to town as quickly as possible.

In the hut where they were staying, Eshen-Kareg cared for his son himself. Calling on his extensive knowledge and carefully selecting herbs and drugs from his own stock, he prepared his son a medicinal tonic. Everyone present was surprised by the father's such attentive devotion but Eshen-Kareg didn't care about other people's perceptions. Yusuf was the most important person in his life and he would do anything to protect him. Eshen-Kareg did not dare to admit even to himself, that he placed too much hope in his son. In his heart, he could not bear to lose him.

Yusuf's two older brothers, long familiar with their father's overprotective attitude towards Yusuf, grinned as they watched all the fuss and growing bored, asked if they could go for a walk around the city.

"Don't go far. Go and see the fair, and then come straight back. And bring some food back with you," asked Eshen-Kareg, before returning to care for Yusuf.

The hut's owner was an elderly woman with kind eyes, wearing the traditional peasant costume of a loose sarafan dress and embroidered white blouse, with a knotted kerchief over her head. She was a secret Old Believer who also attended the Orthodox Church on Sundays.

"I noticed, my dear," commented Eshen-Kareg, "that you pray in secret, out of sight of everyone. Can your faith be so reprehensible that you have to hide it from the community?"

"Do you know, my dear guest Eshen-Kareg," answered the landlady, taking from the oven a clay pot containing steaming cabbage soup, "our faith does not cause anyone harm, after all, there is but one God, but not everyone is as tolerant as you! We old believers have openly accepted Orthodoxy but we still cling to our old faith.

"You are right, Svetlana, and I do understand your position." agreed Eshen-Kareg, accepting his hostess' invitation to join him for dinner.

The stove stood in the centre of the spacious hut which had two small windows through which a light breeze caused the curtains to flutter. On the table, beside the pot of soup, wooden plates and spoons, a vase of flowers which had been plucked by the landlady that morning, filled the room with the fresh, fragrant scent of the departing summer.

"And you, my dear guest, which faith do you follow?" the landlady asked in return.

"We are Muslims. In my country, we originally practised Shamanism and then after Genghis Khan's arrival, Buddhism. But you are right, we all pray to one God!" answered Eshen-Kareg with a smile.

Eating together, they spoke long about the life and traditions of the Russian people.

By evening Yusuf felt better and sat down to eat with the others. The older brothers came back from the fair, bringing a prepared meal as well as provisions for the clerks and chroniclers who had stayed behind in the settlement.

"So, tell us what you saw in the city!" Eshen-Kareg asked his sons.

Ibragim and Sadyk talked excitedly about how much fun they had had in the square, watching the duels of warriors and the loud, drunken fights which followed. There had also been an execution but the brothers hadn't discovered who it was or what they had done.

"Well, let's now give thanks to this house and our kind hostess. We get up early in the morning to return to work in Alexander's settlement" announced Eshen-Kareg.

When everybody had gone to sleep and while their hostess bustled around the house tidying up, he sat down and wrote a petition to the Tsar requesting a transfer for him and two of his sons to the main chamber, arguing that they could just as easily continue with their work on indexing the library from there. He also recommended that his younger son Yusuf would be more useful to the Tsar if he were assigned to teach the children of Moscow's boyars and nobles.

***

Soon Eshen-Kareg received confirmation from the Tsar's office that his request had been granted, and Yusuf would be allowed to teach and conduct other educational work with the children of the city's nobility.

"Yusuf, my boy, come here!" called Eshen-Kareg to his son happily.

As he stood and bowed before his father, Eshen-Kareg then presented his son with the letter containing an invitation to enter the service of the Tsar in Moscow, stamped with the royal seal.

Yusuf would never forget the appalling conditions which they had all endured while working in the oppressive library vaults: the musty odours, the constant damp, the clanking sound of the printing presses the claustrophobia and the employees' waxen faces rasping coughs. He would also carry with him, the suspicion that they were continuously under surveillance by spies paid by the Tsar to eavesdrop on their conversations and discussions. Ever philosophical, his father had never tried to dispel this fear, warning him instead of the need for caution since all walls have eyes and ears. .. This explanation did little to appease Yusuf who deep down, was convinced that the day would come when they would all be entombed between these sinister walls and leaving no trace, their very existence would be forever forgotten.

Chapter IX

The Love and Flight of Yusuf

Yusuf was a handsome and well-built youth of average height, with a high forehead, intelligent eyes and blond hair. He drew attention from girls from all around; the Alexander Settlement, Moscow and then, Ivan the Terrible's royal palace.

Wherever Yusuf went, he was never without a particular notebook, bound in ragged brown leather... No-one knew what it contained and neither the storage workers nor the state officials, who visited the Library to monitor progress, took any notice of it. The notebook was a kind of catalogue book in which he and his father secretly logged records of particular books, delivered to the Library for either its collections or to be edited prior to being reprinted.

New arrivals were regularly sent on to palace where they were voraciously, and critically, read by the Tsar before being stored in the Library. This allowed him to not only expand his broad and varied academic knowledge but also, provided him with the opportunity to censor any content which displeased him! On such occasions, he would personally remove passages and dictate changes to his scribes before ordering the original manuscripts to be burned. New versions were then printed in the basement and added to the Library collections.

Well aware of this practice and able to identify which volumes would be prone to censorship, Eshen-Kareg would endeavour whenever possible, to save and secretly hide the originals whilst ensuring that the Tsar's abridged versions sat on the shelves.

Yusuf, at his father's behest, did not let the secret journal out of his sight, ardently protecting its priceless data on all of the books which had been altered and other, equally valuable references to the works of ancient philosophers which had survived the mists of time.

"My son, here are the records of the wonderful books which I and my trusted friend Deacon Dmitri wish to send to a distant land where they will be safe," said Yusuf's father in one of the rare moments when they were alone. "In due course, I will give you a letter to be inserted into the catalogue book. Written in code, by the Deacon and me, it will specify the country and place to which our precious cargo should be sent."

"There can be little delay! You will have recognised the fact that the Tsar's behaviour is becoming more and more erratic since the arrival of his latest confidante and it is my greatest fear that the potions administered by that scheming witch-sorceress will alter his mind to such an extent that he will be driven to eradicate the entire literary heritage under our care!"

Eshen-Kareg was referring to a "healer" who had gained the Tsar's trust by persuading him of her powers to treat his various illnesses. On several occasions but to no avail, Eshen-Kareg had offered the Tsar his own medicines, sure in the knowledge that his preparations would help the Tsar more than the witch's sorcery. It was rumoured that she regularly brought bowls of green worms into the royal chambers, under the pretext that they were needed to treat his ailing blood vessels. Nobody knew for sure what the worms were or how they differed from the leeches more commonly used but it was obvious that along with a slight improvement in his health, the Tsar had succumbed to greater and wilder eruptions of uncontrollable rage, often leading to the executions of members of his entourage.

Eshen-Kareg himself had observed that during these periods, the Tsar also reached the peak of his "intellectual nihilism", which expressed itself in a methodical eradication of scholarly texts by respected thinkers of antiquity and the substitution with his own "demonic" interpretations. He recorded all data in his secret catalogue book.

"I beg you father, do not worry so," soothed Yusuf, concocting a homemade remedy to calm his father's rising blood pressure. "No-one has the power to stop what she's doing, making it all the more important that you continue logging records of the 'reworked' books and saving the originals from being destroyed. For my part, I promise to do everything possible to ensure that your secret journal never falls into the hands of our enemies, and that the books are saved for the rest of humanity. I give you my pledge and promise that if necessary, I will devote my life to attaining this mission!"

***

Once ensconced in his new teaching post, Yusuf became aware that all aspects of life and work in the Tsar's palace were targets of a multitude of different layers and levels of corruption, intrigue and controversy. The majority of the members of Court and their entourages appeared to be spies and were being spied upon, as individuals acted on the instruction of either the Tsar or others in their quest for power and supremacy. Once an openly happy if somewhat naïve, young man, Eshen-Kareg's youngest son now learnt to become more guarded and restrained in both his actions and his speech. He quickly realised that rumours and slander were the most poisonous and lethal weapons that could be used against anyone, and that those he considered loyal friends could in fact be his most dangerous enemies.

Every morning while passing through the nobles' chambers, Yusuf was conscious of barely audible comments from the servants, sometimes full of praise and admiration but often, more hostile in tone, fuelled by their jealousy of his position. Despite their efforts, Yusuf refused to rise to their taunts and instead, quietly focused on undertaking his teaching duties with utmost dignity and professionalism.

The stifling atmosphere and the repetitive schedule, coupled with loneliness and frustration, made Yusuf feel like his life had become an ever decreasing and endless circle. His young soul was restless and he longed to escape the enclosure of thick stone walls and all that sickened him; especially the people who intensely disliked him and his father and brothers. Yusuf knew perfectly well that his father was also having a hard time but at least he was able to find solace from the human indolence which surrounded him, in his passion for his work and quest to rescue the rare scrolls and lost books, which together, they secreted into the custody of Deacon Dimitriy at the Alexander Settlement.

Yusuf was sure that there had to be some way of escaping their predicament and depressed by the notion that they were destined to spend the rest of their lives in the palace, impatiently nagged his father about what they should do. In the back of his mind, however, there lingered the alarming image from his dream of a long and endless journey into unfamiliar territories.

"Yusuf, you're young, ambitious and full of courage. But remember, this is neither the time nor the place to do anything rash!" his father cautioned him in a whisper.

"I know, Father! But that dream continues to haunt me. I'm sure that something terrible is going to happen!"

"That's enough, son. Enough! Things could be much worse. Now, get on with your work" interjected Eshen-Kareg, worried that Yusuf's frustration would lead to their being banished from the Library and in all likelihood, physically punished. His venerable academic reputation would be ruined but more importantly, if dismissed from the post of Curator of the Imperial Library, he would effectively be forced to abandon his lifelong vocation to conserve rare records of antiquarian philosophies for prosperity. He regarded his appointment by the Tsar as a gift of fate and was not prepared to relinquish it lightly.

Little did either of them realise how much things would change in the next few days…

***

The next day, Yusuf resumed his teaching, anticipating yet another uninspiring session with the nobles' children, but when he looked around the classroom, his heart missed a beat. There in front of his very eyes, was the familiar sweet face, which first glimpsed in the royal carriage, had become engraved in his heart. Momentarily arrested by those sad blue eyes, Yusuf stood in the middle of the chamber, lost for words and barely breathing…

Looking away, he fought to regain his composure, but as the lesson progressed, he took the opportunity to observe his new pupil more carefully. The girl was seventeen years old and finely dressed in red silk and a white cape. She seemed a conscientious pupil but suddenly, as she raised her head from her work, their eyes met and although her face blushed in embarrassment, her gaze revealed a quiet satisfaction that he had noticed her.

His new pupil was named Daria and she really was the illegitimate daughter of the Tsar.

Yusuf found it increasingly difficult to concentrate on his teaching and desperate, asked his father to brew one of his infusions to help focus his mind. Eshen-Kareg was unaware of the cause of the problem but quietly brewed the herbal tea without asking any questions.

However, although Eshen-Kareg understood that his son was now an adult with a right to privacy, he was concerned that Yusuf might be hiding something which could place them all in danger. So one evening after work, before the family sat down to dinner, Eshen-Kareg decided to ask his youngest son what was bothering him.

Yusuf immediately understood what was in store and decided to seize the initiative.

"I know that you're worried about me, father, but there's no need! I am working diligently and in any case, the guards never take their eyes off me! But how are you? Are you worried, as I am, about the long-term future of the Library? Ever since we left the Alexander Settlement I haven't lost this strange feeling. I have the sense that somehow the walls of the storage cellar are forever closing in, and that its location will lost for many long years. Perhaps the disappearance of the library will be brought about by that so-called healer that is constantly at the Tsar's side? Her presence is evil and the damage that she'll cause will be irreparable…"

"Hush, boy!" exclaimed Eshen-Kareg. "Think about what you're saying! And above all, think about whether you need to voice out loud whatever is in your mind. How many times do I have to remind you: even these walls have ears! You've suffered from an overactive imagination since birth. It is imperative that we put aside all our doubts, misgivings and fears, and concentrate on the work to which we have been entrusted. Please understand that there is now nothing more important than this!

"When the Golden Horde collapsed, I had no idea how we would survive. Many of my friends' lives were reduced to abject poverty. If it had not been for my academic success, what would have become of us? What could we have done? Would we have had any chance of survival?

"Almost everything that Genghis Khan achieved was destroyed afterwards by his former henchmen and the dark clans are now trying to obliterate anything that remained…" Here Eshen-Kareg stopped, realising that in his agitated state, he too had become guilty of stating aloud fears about issues which were uppermost in his thoughts. Now silent, he sat staring at the smouldering fire in the hearth with eyes which conveyed an inescapable sorrow.

Yusuf's own emotional turmoil was instantly abated…

That night Yusuf did not sleep but lay fantasising about meeting the dawn somewhere far from the palace walls and running into the forest where free at last, he could shout and sing, and swim in a river…

Towards daybreak he sneaked past the palace guard and disappeared from the palace for the whole day, abandoning his lessons.

Eshen-Kareg waited anxiously for his son until late that evening. But when Yusuf returned home excited and beaming with happiness, everything became clear: he realised that his son was a grown man and in love. He also understood that it meant the end of their time in the service of Tsar Ivan.

Eshen-Kareg did not rebuke his son and did not dare to disturb his spiritual joy and happiness. He knew that Yusuf could not remain forever under his wing and that the day would come when Yusuf broke free and with his God-given independent nature, love of freedom and bright mind, would pursue his own aspirations and search for a better life.

"Who is she?" he asked softly.

"She is my life's dream" Yusuf averted his eyes. His cheeks twitched nervously. Yusuf longed to share his feelings with his father and tell him about his love for the woman whom he had been meeting in secret but since their relationship was in principle impossible, he knew that he had to be very careful about what he said.

Eshen-Kareg was happy and sad for his son; glad that he had found love but distraught by the inevitable dangers which it imposed, should it ever become public knowledge. It was now imperative that they leave the area as soon as possible.

Taking immediate action, he wrote a letter to the Tsar the very next morning requesting a transfer for him and his sons to take up similar work in Arkhangelsk.

Anticipating that the old man might instigate such radical measures, Yusuf's fears were confirmed when he read the letter, still unsealed on his father's desk. Since the prospect of being parted from Daria was too unbearable to contemplate, he therefore arranged to intercept the letter before it reached the Tsar and following the servant on route to the state chancellery, persuaded him to join him for a drink and a meal in the tavern. He then replaced the letter with one which he had forged in his father's handwriting. Instead of a request for a transfer, the second letter outlined an argument for a raise in Eshen-Kareg's salary…

A few weeks later, Eshen-Kareg was summoned to the state chancellery, expecting to hear news about his transfer. He was astonished to hear nothing on this subject and was further puzzled by a statement outlining reasons why his wage would not be increased, and the presentation of a gold medallion awarded for his services to the Tsar of all Russia.

The medal was two-sided, and in two parts. On one side was an engraving of the royal crown inlaid with yellow gemstones and framed by a garland of laurel. Inscribed along the lower edge were the words: "Eshen-Kareg: Valiant Librarian to the Russian Sovereign"

On the reverse, was an engraved head of the Tsar and the inscription "The First Russian Emperor of Moscow. Also, unusually, there were small indentations which marked points at which the medallion could be opened to reveal secret compartments.

This unusual and unexpected gift left Eshen-Kareg deeply confused. He could not understand whether it was an act of spontaneous generosity by the Tsar or a subtle way of appeasing him for the decision against his transfer.

In any case, Eshen-Kareg's plans for his son had now been scuppered and it was only a matter of time before each member of his family would receive severe punishment for Yusuf's clandestine relationship with the Tsar's illegitimate daughter. In the vain hope that the Court remained oblivious to the affair, Eschen-Kareg tried to arrange an audience with the Tsar in order to thank him personally for his kindness and also clarify the situation by renewing his request for a transfer. However, with the exception of meetings attended by both the Tsar and Eschen-Kareg concerning negotiations with envoys from the southern and eastern borders of Great Russ, no such opportunities arose.

Heedful of the need to keep his feelings of impending gloom well hidden, Eshen-Kareg decided to celebrate his receipt of the medallion with his sons and his colleagues and organised a party in a local tavern.

Although Yusuf had missed the camaraderie of the Library workers, he felt too despondent to join in the revelry and instead, quietly concentrated on the design of the extravagant royal gift.

"Look father; there are faint markings on one side of the medallion that show how separate parts of its body can be opened. This is a remarkable piece of craftsmanship! Fascinated, he continued to explore the medallion's miniature mechanism.

"There are lots of secret compartments in its body, you say? Let's have a look – will there be one big enough to hide our map in?" and Eshen-Kareg looked at his son pointedly.

"Come on then, let's have a look at the Tsar's present." Sadyk sat down beside his younger brother and taking the medallion, he began to turn it around in his hands, staring at the arrows. Following the direction of one of them he pulled at a tiny lever at the point where the two main parts of the body joined. With a light click, a tiny leather strap was revealed but unable to work out its function, Sadyk decided that it probably didn't work and so returned the lever to its original position.

All of a sudden, a bright bluish flame was emitted from the medallion, momentarily illuminating the faces of everyone at the table. Startled, Yusuf could have sworn that instead of seeing their usual facial features, the mysterious light exposed the contours of their skulls with gaping eye sockets and bare jaws.

There then came a fierce flash of fire which set alight the hem of the hem of Sadyk's shirt. Shocked, he immediately dropped the medallion and yelling, darted through the room. Seized by panic, the rest of the party followed suit until taking control of the situation, Deacon Dimitriy, threw a large bucket of water over Sadyk to extinguish the flames. Once they realised that the danger had passed, everyone began to laugh uproariously, recharged their drinks and resumed their noisy celebrations.

It seemed that the only person who remained greatly disturbed by the incident was Eschen-Kareg, who sober and serious, stood to address the party: "Well, my children, the wise ones say that fire should never be trifled with and after tonight's event, I have no choice but to return this medallion to its owner"

With these words, the library curator picked up the medallion from where it had fallen under the table and carefully wiping it ensured that all of its moveable parts were returned to their original positions. Later, when he was certain that the guests were once again engrossed in their tipsy banter, Eshen-Kareg took from his pocket a tightly rolled miniature map and carefully placed it in one of the hidden sections of the medallion which he then hung around his neck. The party continued until the early hours of the morning and even Sadyk, once he had changed into dry clothes, was able to laugh off his embarrassment and make light of the incident.

***

They met secretly and spent many hours together near the deep and roaring river, which flowed between the birch trees and green fields. As Daria sat in the cool shade weaving dandelion wreaths, Yusuf could hardly keep his eyes off his beloved, savouring every curve of her slender body and her eyes which were more beautiful than dawn. Neither knew just how fleeting their time would be together but their mutual passion drove them to bouts of fervent kissing, leaving their lips red and swollen. As they grew to know each other more intimately, they became less self-conscious and the fear and shame of their relationship, rooted in their disobedience of their fathers, all but disappeared.

"Yusuf, I cannot leave here without you," said Daria suddenly, as her hot tears fell on her lover's shoulder.

Yusuf soothed her and held her closer, saying:

"Don't worry, Daryushka: everything will go according to God's will. We will definitely be together – I have a plan…"

"Yusuf – you can't imagine what my father would do to you if he found out about us. It's not for nothing that they call him 'the Terrible'. His wild jealousy and vindictive nature, the ambition and pride which torment him and the hold which that witch has over him, make him monstrous and violent. He will do everything in his power to ruin you, my dear, my love and he will have no hesitation in killing both of us!" Daria sobbed uncontrollably.

"Do not cry, my dear, my heart has been torn in pieces and only you can mend it. My soul will always belong to you, I swear! ...We'll find a way to stay together but right now we must return! There must have been three changes of guards since we left the class this morning and suspicions will be raised by our absence."

"I know.... Our union has been my destiny since my childhood ... We must embrace it and never let it go!"

The lovers' conversation was suddenly interrupted by a light easterly wind which carried the sound of cracking twigs and then closer by, a strangled cry. At that moment Yusuf's older brothers – Ibragim and Sadyk – appeared before them in a state of confusion.

"What have you done, Yusuf? You've delivered a sentence of death upon us all!!!" spluttered Ibragim with pure hatred, as he threw down a sack containing monk's robes. "Get changed, the horses are waiting. We need to leave immediately! The Tsar's guards have been instructed to hunt you down and our father has been arrested! Knowing that you would ignore his warnings and growing increasingly anxious about your behaviour, he has been anticipating this outcome for some time and asked us to keep an eye on you. He had also made preparations for our escape."

With these words, Ibragim strode off in the direction of a body of one of the Tsar's guards sprawled on the ground.

"There were two of them... but one managed to escape!" finished Ibragim, gloomily.

"Oh Lord have mercy! Lord have mercy!" wailed Daria in terror.

"Shut up!" shouted Ibragim. "Follow the creek to the west. About half a mile from here, near the broom bush, father's friend Deacon Dmitriy will meet you. He will take you back to the palace. You won't be allowed out until the ship arrives to take you to your fiancé in one of the far northern countries. Take the dungeon key: you must use it to get to our father and let him know we managed to escape.

With these words, Ibragim stretched over to give the poor girl a small key.

"Right, time to hit the road!" announced Sadyk, helping Yusuf into his saddle.

"Dear, dear Yusuf!" cried Daria, with bitter tears.

"Time's up! Forget your goodbyes. Let's go!" Sadyk turned and whipped Yusuf's horse.

And so Ibragim and Sadyk sped away with her lover, leaving an inconsolable Daria alone with her grief and the body of the strangled guard. In a daze and rocked by her grief, she walked along the creek towards Deacon Dmitriy who managed to smuggle her, unseen, into the imperial palace.

The brothers fled further and further east, prudently covering their trail. They travelled only at night and by day, hid themselves deep in the dense cover of the forests. The long road ahead promised to be full of difficulties and disappointments.

***

The Tsar's anger was terrible to behold and his rage reached new heights when the guards consigned to capture the fugitives, returned with only the body of the murdered, imperial spy.

He immediately descended to the dungeon where Eshen-Kareg, bloody and exhausted after being brutally tortured, now sat under heavy guard.

"I trusted you with my state affairs! But you, you devil, calamitous Nogoy! Well!" Seized by an uncontrollable burst of anger, the Tsar seized Eshen-Kareg by his beard and began to slam the old man's head against the cell's stone walls.

Eshen-Kareg bravely accepted all the blows that fate threw at him, knowing he would not be spared. One of the guards splashed his face with cold water and he slowly regained consciousness following the severe beating. Supporting his broken ribs, he was led away to the Chamber where his trial was to commence.

Turning to Tsar, he spoke in a quiet but firm voice:

"Sovereign; I willingly came to your palace at your request and invested all of my time and knowledge in the creation of a Library. Under my guidance, many other employees and scribes also committed a great deal of energy in the achievement of your goal. I have served you well, have I not?"

Ignoring this comment, the Tsar furiously scanned the faces of all those seated in the room before turning to Eschen-Kareg.

"Tell me: How did this heathen- devil Yusuf get away from under my very nose?"

"Any father would do everything he could to ensure his son's freedom and survival. Anyone would have done the same in my place, and it is not treachery, my Lord Tsar!" responded Eshen-Kareg evenly.

Growling and pacing the room like a tiger, the Tsar lost all patience and loudly summoned his guards.

"Do not take your eyes of him! Tomorrow I will set him the cruellest punishment."

With clenched teeth and bulging eyes, he then grabbed one of the terrified guards, lifting him from the floor.

"Go and catch this devil Yusuf! I need him alive, do you hear, alive! I will fry his liver!"

Nogoy – Tatar.

Explosive with rage, he threw the guard aside and marched out of the room, slamming the door behind him.

***

Deacon Dmitry had managed to bring Daria secretly to her chambers. On the way she cried girlish tears, hugging the Deacon's shoulders. Now she sat at her window. And when the Tsar burst in on her, roaring and shouting, Daria met her father with a look that was calm and fearless.

This seemed to have a restorative effect on the Tsar, and he came to his senses, seeing his adult and independent daughter standing before him with a reproachful gaze.

"Daryushka, my daughter!" The Tsar suddenly fell to his knees and burst into loud tears. He understood that her imperious character in many ways resembled his own. Here was grown and spirited woman was standing before him.

At a certain level he was enraptured with his daughter. He concealed these feelings deep inside.

"Father, do not cry!" exclaimed Daria. "You are the Tsar for the people, but for me you are just my father! You are always so busy with your dissolute and cruel life. Soon that boat will arrive for me, and you will never see me again. I forgive you!"

"Have mercy on your father!" He cried even louder, like a bashful child.

Daria looked intently at her father with a wry smile on her lips as she whispered softly in his ear:

"Father, listen to Eshen-Kareg's advice. My heart senses that the Witch is up to no good."

"Ah! But will you not tell me where that heathen brat Yusuf has run too?" whispered the Tsar, in a now malicious tone of voice.

"You will learn nothing from me! The grave will not cure the

122

hunchback!" Darya responded in the same spirit of resistance.

"Guards! Guards! Before the ship arrives, this young lady is going nowhere! Do you hear me: Nowhere!" Screaming loudly and slamming the door behind him, the Tsar poked the guard in the forehead with his index finger, scaring him close to death.

This was the last meeting between Daria and her father Ivan the Terrible.

***

Night had fallen… Through a small window shone a corner of the waning moon. Eshen- Kareg took this as a sign that all his sins were absolved. These thoughts calmed him as he sat in his dark dungeon waiting for morning and his execution.

Now he understood the roots of all of the anxieties which his son Yusuf had experienced in his dreams and premonitions and had repeatedly tried to warn his father about.

But Eshen-Kareg felt no regret: he had learned from his faithful friend Deacon Dmitry that his sons had managed to elude the Tsar's chase. Yusuf, Sadyk and Ibrahim had escaped across the river and covered their tracks very carefully…

A quiet rustling noise interrupted Eshen-Kareg's thoughts. And then a voice, like the sound of a morning bell, was heard in the prisoner's ear: "Dear sir Eshen-Kareg"

Someone had crept into the dungeon so quietly that all of the guards continued to sleep.

Eshen-Kareg squinted in the darkness and saw Daria, dressed in a monastic habit. Her sad blue eyes were consumed with anxiety and determination.

"What are you doing here? If the guards find you here we will both be executed," whispered Eshen-Kareg, in a stern voice.

Forgive me, my dear Eshen-Kareg! Everything is my fault. Will Yusuf forgive me?" Daria continued in a quiet but imploring voice.

"Calm down, my dear. What's got into you?" Eshen-Kareg tried to soothe her.

"Stop wasting your tears. You are young, your... love burns and throbs, and no-one has the power to outshine it – even the Tsar himself," he said, with a wry smile on his face.

He then asked Daria for one big favour:

"In my chambers you will find a wooden trunk. There's a liquid in there that will help me sleep forever. Do not torment your young soul; do not punish yourself. Your love for Yusuf will help him survive, even at the most difficult moments in his life. You know, he always tried to warn me. He wanted to tell me about his dreams. But I was an old fool and did not listen to him as I should have. Well... We cannot change our fate."

"Sir, wherever I will live, your bloodline will live too. Yusuf's child – your grandson – is growing in my womb," said Daria, in a beseeching whisper.

Eshen-Kareg quietly sobbed to himself. Rubbing away his old-man's tears, he blessed Daria and gave her the first part of the gold medallion. He explained that Yusuf had the second part, as well as the priceless catalogue book that contained all of the data which he had compiled.

"It seems that this medallion was made by a very talented master goldsmith, who had a very clear idea of the importance of my mission." His eyes sparkled with hope. Whispering, he calmly continued:

"I can't explain it in ordinary words. The mechanism behind this medallion has very interesting features. The two parts can be separated and even used individually. That's why I gave the second part to Yusuf: he will be able to use it in the very difficult times that lie ahead of him: the simple mechanism inside it can help him create fire. The first part, with the precious stone, has magical properties. When I joined the two parts together, I discovered clues to its real secret.

"I used the special light which emanates from the precious stone to write the catalogue - and it is only by this light that the information can be read with ease."

"Deacon Dmitry has managed to smuggle all of the invaluable books onto the ship that will take you far from here," he added, looking into the far distance.

As Daria listened to the old man telling this far-fetched story in his dark prison cell, she secretly believed that he had gone completely mad, yet she continued to nod attentively.

Suddenly, Eshen-Kareg fell silent. He was well aware of how strange this story must sound to Daria, especially since she had no prior knowledge of anything that he was telling her, but it was critical that she understood and accepted the significance of the secrets being unfolded and agree to obey his last wish. He continued talking to her in a more familiar tone:

"Please believe me when I say that I have no regrets, my daughter. You have made me a very happy old man. May the Almighty protect you and my grandson. The rare books will prove very precious for all of humanity. There are two maps: Yusuf has a second copy of the country for which your ship is bound. My work for the Tsar was not in vain! I secretly discovered your location and drew your path by the stars. Take great care of all your valuable cargo. There is nothing I can do to escape the Tsar's rage and my execution but I can now rest in peace knowing that you and Yusuf will survive and the story will live on…"

Daria went to fetch what he had requested and seeing Yusuf's silver lamp on his father's table, kissed the second part of the locket before folding and hiding the map next to her heart. She delivered the medicine and shedding tears of sorrow, said goodbye forever to Eshen-Kareg. Daria then returned to her chamber to await the arrival of the ship which would take her on the most enigmatic of journeys.

On discovering the next day that Eshen-Kareg had already entered an eternal sleep, the Tsar had the two guards beheaded, since neither could explain why the old man had not survived another day.

Once something has happened, it cannot be reversed and if unabated, can spark off a trail of destruction which cannot be halted.

One day whilst on important business in Alexander Settlement, the Tsar in an enraged and deranged state of mind accidentally killed his son and everything that Yusuf had predicted and worried about came true. The Witch used "dark powers" to wall up the doors of the Library forever. It is said that no traces of the Library have been found to this day and the mystery of its disappearance remains to be solved.

***

One road: Three riders. Often travelling through the darkness and reading the stars to find their way, Yusuf and his brothers continued on their journey. They were following the map that Yusuf had received from his father but this was the same long, endless road which Yusuf had seen often in his dreams…

Rising early one morning, Ibrahim and Sadyk were enjoying a dramatic sunrise when they became aware of Yusuf screaming and whimpering like a dog in his sleep. It was as if their younger brother was losing his mind.

"Don't punish yourself, Yusuf," said Sadyk slapping him on his shoulder. "You knew what was coming. You knew what the consequences would be. May father rest in eternal sleep. Amen, Stop tearing yourself apart. Don't let yourself be driven mad by it all. Do you hear me?"

"Sadyk, I will never find peace. My soul will be searching for eternity. And I cannot forgive myself. Father doted on me!" Yusuf suddenly burst into tears.

"Be quiet! Bloody well control yourself and shut up!" retorted Sadyk angrily. "It's time for you to act like a grown man!"

They always argued about who would perform necessary duties, but that day, Sadyk went quietly to the river to get water before announcing that he would go back to sleep until it was time to move on at nightfall.

This allowed Yusuf peaceful time alone in which to study the map that his father had given him and explore once more, the gold medallion and its internal mechanism. As he did so, he recalled that night in the tavern and the expressions on the scribes' faces as they all witnessed the flames which had erupted from this extraordinary instrument.

The map has been created using a particular geometric layout which could only be read with the second portion of the medallion. The need to decipher all of these occult symbols on the posts and the diagonals affirmed the medallion's mysterious qualities and induced in Yusuf, a sense that the message hidden behind the symbols would not be unravelled until some point in the distant future.

"I need to examine every part of it carefully and then draw up a plan or even hide this half of the medallion alongside this card somewhere. Whoever finds them would then need to look for the second part in order to discover its deepest secrets," whispered Yusuf to himself.

The two brothers, deeply concerned about Yusuf's mental state decided to leave him alone to study his precious catalogue book bound in brown leather.

Their long journey had now led them to a place where the dunes of the desert rolled far beyond the horizon and where the going was so arduous that it felt as if time stood still.

As they trudged over the ever shifting, fine golden sand, their eyes smarted and the exhausting heat of the day forced them to seek camel thorn, so that they could quench their thirst by drinking the juices from its roots. For food, they hunted for snakes or lizards. And so the days passed…

***

After many days of silence, they were greatly relieved to hear the sound of animals' bells from an approaching caravan and it would be this which would guarantee salvation for the three fugitives.

"Where have you come from?" asked the leader, a trustworthy Kazakh bii, who was travelling home with expensive goods.

"We are sons of a Nogoy bii who served in Muscovy (Moscow). Our father was executed but we were helped to escape. We are now in search of new lands," replied Ibrahim, the eldest brother.

"Well then, you're in luck! This route is too long and hard to be travelling alone. You can join the caravan and serve me by helping to care for my camels and horses." proposed the Kazakh bii with a kind smile.

Days, weeks and then months passed until the caravan reached its destination.

One fine morning the brothers woke up to find that the caravan and the Kazakh had disappeared without a trace.

They were surrounded by an eerie silence and all that remained of the caravan were deposits of manure.

"How on earth did they manage to set off without making a sound? Why have they abandoned us and left us here alone?" Sadyk, the middle brother paced to and for anxiously, still in a state of disbelief in what had happened.

Deep feelings of resentment were causing his cheekbones to twitch nervously and his eyes betrayed his anger and desperation.

"Don't get so upset, Sadyk. We no longer need each other! We helped him to cross the most difficult part of the desert, and in exchange he did not leave use to die in the desert sand. No wonder he plied us so generously with wine yesterday!" said Yusuf, trying to reassure his brother.

"Why do you say we don't need him anymore? He promised me that I would marry one of his daughters. He promised me some land, and a job!" screamed Sadyk, loudly and hysterically.

"Don't you understand, Sadyk! We served him and in return he helped us to navigate the long and difficult journey. That's it! "

"Oh you... It's all because of you! Our father was executed because of you! It's your fault we are in these foreign lands! This is all your fault!" shouted Sadyk, losing his temper. "The Kazakh bii noticed you flirting with his young concubine! He is not blind!"

"I did not flirt with his concubine! Are you out of your mind?! Only Daria, my love, resides in my heart. Yes, I can't forgive myself for the fact that it was it was my fault that Father was executed! Yes, it will haunt me my whole life. But you are naïve!" retorted Yusuf in self-defence.

"Why can't you live quietly? Accept life as it is, like everyone else instead of looking for trouble? You are a demon and a tyrant!" Fuelled by his anger and despair, Sadyk leapt towards his younger brother in a violent attack.

"Let's tie him up and leave him here in the desert: this devil will die alone!" shouted Sadyk.

Ibrahim, long frustrated by Yusuf's behaviour, joined Sadyk in beating up their younger brother. Outnumbered, any attempts at retaliation were futile but as they were tying him up, Yusuf remembered something his father had taught him in childhood and could almost hear his voice whispering in his ear: "You need to make a tight fist and not let it go. After they tighten the rope you will be able to straighten your fingers, which will give you space. If you rub your hands together you can free yourself. Remember, my son..."

Amidst the pain of being so brutally by his brothers, Yusuf who had curled himself up in a ball to deflect some of the blows heard only that voice.

He couldn't understand what had triggered this act of such violent hatred. His own blood, his brothers whom he loved unconditionally, wished him dead! They had left him, bound, bruised and bleeding in torn clothes to die alone in the desert.

Fortunately had been in such a rush to tie him up that they had failed to notice his clenched fist....

Yusuf lay moaning in pain for many hours, passing in and out of consciousness. He was only able to open one eye. As darkness fell, he opened his clenched fist and slowly and painfully, managed to free himself from the ropes before blacking out again.

Between his waking hours and dreams he heard a voice, disconnected to any physical being yet as clear as if someone were standing beside him whispering softly in his ear:

"You have to continue our bloodline, Yusuf…" The voice then changed and continued with a laugh, preventing him from fully losing consciousness. What was it? A vision? …

***

Yusuf's dream

Was it a dream? Or reality? … Perhaps elements from his previous life… Clouds forming a particular image… Those familiar eyes, that pleasant smile – this image would accompany Yusuf for his whole life.

A light breeze caused the sand to whirl up, slowly changing its form and drawing the eyes of the solitary traveller. Yusuf tried to see something in it. The vast expanse of the sky stretched on to infinity. He tried to remember some details.

"Daria???" he suddenly tried to shout out as loud as he could. But the vague shape just shimmered in the air, appearing and then disappearing.

Yusuf would long paint in his mind those secret meetings, seeing his first love and her smile. His ardour and tender love, the secret they coveted and hid from everyone around them. He recounted the times when the atmosphere had been heavy with youthful temptation … Yusuf breathed deeply and tried to inhale her fragrance and relive moments when he caressed her delicate shoulders and covered her with tender kisses as gentle as a morning flower.

Over and over again, the sound of voices prohibited him from losing consciousness: "Yusuf, you must continue our bloodline…"

Yusuf remembered these hours of solitude forever and they were always accompanied by thoughts and memories of Daria.

He whispered to himself:

> "Daria, I will live by your love,
> I will look for it everywhere.
> Each of us has their own destiny,
> Through your eyes, I will see the world…"

As another night approached, Yusuf set aside the leather bound catalogue book which was all that was left of everything he had held most dear, and roused himself to gather up manure. Using the mechanism in the medallion was able to light a fire.

Thus began his solitary survival in the desert and as his strength returned, he was gradually able to hunt and feed himself on marmots and lizards.

His thoughts were in the clouds and soon Yusuf lost all sense of the passing of time.

One day, on waking from a nap, he sensed a presence and was surprised to see a hunter towering above him.

"So you're alive?" With a grin, the stranger dismounted from his horse, and began to ask Yusuf several questions.

"First, give me some water to drink, stranger," begged Yusuf, in a hoarse voice. He was still half asleep.

"Where are you heading?" Having provided food and water, the hunter conversed with Yusuf for a long time and was astonished by the story being told by this lonely figure.

"We ran from the grand palace; my father Eshen-Kareg, was executed but my brothers and I were able to escape."

"And why are you now here and all alone? Where are your brothers;

what happened to them?" asked the hunter.

"We argued here and my brothers betrayed me. They tied me up, beat me and left me to die in the desert," answered Yusuf gloomily.

"How could that be? You look like such an intelligent man, but they left you alone? Ay-ay, you were born under a lucky star Yusuf. Here it is not customary to leave travellers alone. But sometimes strangers can be kinder than blood relatives. Such is human nature."

"I will not forget your kindness. What can I call you, my friend?"

"My name is Baibolot. I am a grandson of Tagay-Bii, the son of Sayak. Here at the river Ile, I was supposed to divide the Kazakh herd in two," the kind hunter grinned as he spoke.

Baibolot invited Yusuf to travel with him to the northern regions.

"I cannot leave you a here. Come to my region and settle there. You can use your knowledge to teach our children and you may even find yourself a bride." Winking, he helped Yusuf to change into new clothes. The travellers agreed on their new plans and joking loudly with each other, they headed on their way.

And so the two riders headed to the northern regions. On the road they came across the remains of an ancient city.

"What happened here, Baibolot?" asked Yusuf in astonishment.

"It was a flourishing city for several millennia. Burana Tower lit the caravan road. This was once a major trading post but now its ruined remains serve as a reminder that nothing is eternal in this world."

"Here is the home of a most important holy mazar – I must pray." Yusuf dismounted from his horse and fell to his knees at the gate, before turning his gaze to the ruined site beyond the crumbling walls. Under his arm he gripped his father's gift of the priceless catalogue, from which he would not be parted until old age, but it was here that he relinquished his father's other gift, by digging a deep hole and burying the second part of the medallion and its hidden map.

"…May the Almighty assist us in the future, and guide someone to seek and find everything that was precious to my father and me. Let these walls guard the fruits of his labour, under the heavens and stars in this mystical place. Amen."

Yusuf prayed long and hard for his own destiny and that of his future children and grandchildren; for the mystical ways and paths that crossed this place, for his first love, who would live forever in his heart, and for that presence that did not allow him to die in the desert.

With his emaciated and trembling fingers, Yusuf stroked the enormous stones that were carved in honour of three great religions which had lived together in harmony in this city for thousands of years: Islam, Christianity and Buddhism.

The travellers continued onwards: Baibolot, the grandson of Tagay Bii's son of Sayak, and Yusuf, the son of Eshen-Kareg. On arriving in the northern regions, Yusuf became known as Jusup , in keeping with local dialect, but with reference to his saintly appearance and pale blue eyes, he also received a new name: Chekir Moldo the blue-eyed mullah.

He married one of Tagay-Bii's granddaughters, taught local children how to write and lived to an extremely old age. Before passing out of this world, he told his story, and gave the invaluable and precious leather-bound catalogue book to one of his grandsons, in order that he in time would pass both the book and the story on to the next generation.

And that is how the story has survived to this day.

Later the following historical facts would be revealed:

His brother Sadyk found himself in Kazakhstan, where the new "Kyzyl Oruk" line lives on to this day.

His other brother Ibragim went to Talas and started his own line.

Because of his resentment towards his brothers, Yusuf refused to have any contact with Sadyk or Ibrahim.

Mazar- is holy place, often mausoleum and often with ancient saint.

Chapter X

The Castle of the Blackdales Clan

Listening to J.M's narration of this extraordinary story, Dr Silver and his friends were entranced and immediately recognised, its potential as a key to many of the mysteries that Dr Silver and his assistant had spent so long researching in archival records. They rejoiced with childlike enthusiasm, drank some strong coffee and continued on their quest. Such detailed historical details revealed by the story, had unsettled even the stoic Dr Silver.

From time to time J.M. glanced at John Peterson. At such times, neither averted their eyes from the other, and each conducted a wishful dialogue in their imaginations. In their thoughts they walked together through the city at nightfall, each revealing their true feelings...

As it grew late, Dr Silver suggested that they all go to his residence, as the danger had still not passed. The head of the Blackdales was still at large.

"I suggest that we all stick together. J.M, you have a special assignment. Let's go to your place first, where you can collect the valuable catalogue book from your safe. I would like to see it and study it, with your permission of course." Closing the Centre, he called the police. Now the Centre would be under surveillance, in case the head of the Blackdales clan returned.

They left for J.M.'s home.

"You wait in the car while I go into the house, pick up the catalogue and return immediately." Suspecting nothing, J.M. forgot all precautions, as beaming with happiness she entered her stairwell.

To her great astonishment, J.M. heard strange voices. She shrugged her shoulders; her neighbours were usually very quiet people. She wondered if they had been drinking or celebrating something. Why else would anyone be making so much noise this late at night?

Suddenly noticing that the door to her flat was ajar, she became breathless and her heart began to pound in fear. Stepping forward, she surreptitiously peeped past the door, and was perturbed to catch a glimpse of the type of shoes normally worn by Miss McKendry. She then overheard her speaking to someone else about plans to gather essential clues which only J.M. and bald Dr Silver could provide. Only then could they solve the mystery, about which she knew nothing. As for JM and Dr Silver, it would be her pleasure to dispose of them afterwards and she would ensure that no traces would ever be found of their bodies.

Terrified, J.M. automatically stepped back from the entrance to her flat and in so doing, accidentally banged her bag against the wall. Afraid that she had been heard, she tried to make her way as silently and quickly as possible down the dimly-lit stairwell and into the car. Too late! Within seconds, she was grabbed from behind by someone wearing a dark mask who immediately covered her mouth with a rag soaked in a powerful anaesthetic.

Miss JM collapsed unconscious into the arms of the man who had earlier disguised himself as the postman.

Waking up in a darkened minibus, J.M. recognised the man in the dark cloak whom she had seen in the shadows of the Centre and whom she suspected had been following her. The man sat with a wide grin on his face and idly scratched his head as he peered through a thick magnifying glass at both the letter from the antiques dealer and the valuable catalogue.

"You won't be able to work out anything!" shouted J.M. indignantly, realising her complete helplessness.

"Hah! And what do you think you're here for, girl? And in a couple of hours we'll have that old, bald Dr Silver as well. You've a busy time ahead showing me how to find the treasure!" The Blackdales Clan chief laughed malevolently.

The minibus had accelerated and was now travelling at speed: a clear sign that they had long left the city behind...

**

Dr Silver was waiting anxiously, puzzled by the long absence of his assistant. He suggested they go up to J.M.'s flat.

Climbing the stairs, they discovered her door wide open. In addition, the catalogue book had disappeared from her safe, and J.M.'s white scarf was lying on the floor. A huge stubbed out cigar was still emitting a pungent smell. Perhaps someone from the Blackdales Clan had smoked it while waiting for J.M...

"Damn it!" shouted Dr Silver, at a complete loss. His temple was throbbing from the shocking and unexpected turn of events.

"Where could they have taken her, doctor? They used another door, the scoundrels!" John Peterson was pacing up and down the flat.

Rubbing his bald head and fiddling with his horn-rimmed glasses, Dr Silver suddenly had a spark of inspiration.

"Wait a minute – I think I know where these Blackdales vultures are!" He raced down to the car shouting for the driver to take them from the city towards Berwick, the town on the border between Scotland and England, and Black Rock Island, where he believed the Blackdales could be hiding.

"Why did I not think of this before? After all, Mrs Jane McKendry invited us to visit long ago. Did she give away her secret as an oversight?" With one eyebrow raised and a certain feeling of satisfaction despite the shock, Dr Silver watched his friend loading his gun and calling his team on his phone.

"By the way, her mobile phone is in her purse. There are missed calls on it, Dr Silver: you should check to see if there's anything that sounds urgent," said the driver. He was already on the main road and accelerating towards the border.

The missed calls were from Dr Craig Robinson.

"Miss J.M., look for the key word. We have found the second part of the gold medallion, after almost two months of excavations. The medallion is more like a clockwork mechanism. There is also a map, a very old one and you can just about recognise certain symbols and even, numbers. I myself discovered that the word "Eshen" translates from ancient Gaelic as 'at the water' or 'near the water', and so your hypothesis about Yusuf's account appears to be true. These items may lead to the solution. We now need the second part of the medallion. Perhaps, if they are designed to connect to provide a coherent design it will be easier to move the investigation forward. Please call me back as soon as you can…"

"Oh God! Dr Robinson has found the second part of the medallion! What great news!" shouted Dr Silver with joy, having listened to the voice message several times. He was twisting and gnawing at something deep in his thoughts.

John Peterson drew a plan of the island. He nervously typed something into his laptop, and gave someone instructions.

"Wait – do not do anything without us. We'll be there soon and will get in touch," commanded John Peterson.

***

The tide had now fully covered the sandy road to Black Rock Island. To wait for the next low tide would be a complete disaster.

"Here's the boat which I've borrowed from a local fisherman." John Peterson was about to start the engine whilst everyone climbed aboard, when he discovered that it had been savagely perforated with large holes. Disappointed but not entirely surprised, he decided to move on to his alternative plan to reach the island.

"Surely these vultures could have left us with a boat that wasn't damaged?" muttered Dr Silver loudly and unhappily.

"This was to be expected, damn it!" cursed John Peterson repeatedly.

From the car's boot he pulled out scuba diving suits and he instructed his friends to put them on and dive into the water immediately. The waves slowly rocked the swimmers.

"Oh, J.M. has become entrenched deep into your soul, hasn't she?" noted Dr Silver, looking at his friend's stern face with a kind smile.

"One life wouldn't be enough to express my feelings for her. She is very precious to me! Dive into the water my friend," he said, winking at the Doctor.

Having swum to the Black Rock, the friends hid their scuba equipment under some seaweed, loaded their guns and quietly headed inland.

Anxiously awaiting low tide, many tourists were watching the beautiful sunset. Dr Silver, Peterson and his colleagues found it easier to move around, unnoticed, in the crowd of spectators.

They slowly moved around, scanning the island and the faces of the tourists for any leads, until they suddenly noticed an old, and seemingly abandoned, house.

Moving towards it, they heard a voice from the small opening in the wall and without slowing down Peterson nodded and pointed to his colleagues indicating that they should inspect this house carefully and be on alert.

"Jeez, we need to get their attention somehow – do we need to know how many there are?"

"Maybe take one of the tourists hostage and ask for a small favour," suggested Dr Silver in a whisper.

"Excuse me, my friend: tell me you were joking?" Raising an eyebrow, Peterson gave a signal to one of his associates.

"I want to be helpful and give you some sage advice. Sorry it didn't work out right!" Dr Silver apologised for his unsuccessful joke.

Scaring the tourists could have a fatal effect. That might lead the desperate and pitiless Blackdales to kill these innocent people en masse.

"Why don't you," said one of the companions, who had just arrived with a hot pizza, "pretend that you are delivering this pizza by mistake."

They knocked at the door. A few minutes later, someone looked through the slot and asked in a husky voice:

"Who's there? What do you need?"

"You asked for some pizza. We're delivering it," answered the man, who was wearing a red cap.

"We didn't order anything. Go away!" shouted the man, quietly opening the door out of curiosity.

At this very moment the man who stood at the door heard a dull shot.

Peterson and his associates rushed forward and broke down the door.

Someone shouted for help, the muffled sound of a gunshot was heard, someone fell over and someone moaned for help.

"Damn!" shouted Peterson. He asked everyone if they were all right.

"Peterson, I'm here and need help," called a hoarse voice. Dr Silver stood lamely at the door with a wounded leg. Beside him lay a dead, bearded man.

"Someone, please help Dr Silver!" ordered Peterson, who quickly checking the house, found no sign of J.M.

As soon as they had managed to get a boat back to the mainland, Peterson reached for his first aid kit from the car and began to properly examine Dr Silver's wounded leg. He then gave him an injection to help him overcome the shock and recommended that his friend immediately left for the city.

"Miss J.M. and the head of the Blackdales vultures could be in the castle dungeon," he said, applying a bandage to Dr Silver's wound.

"Anything's possible. The old witch is the owner of the castle, under a false name. To divert attention from what really goes on there, she has opened the top part to tourists." Clutching his fist against the pain of his wounds, Dr Silver struggle to continue with what else he wanted to say.

"She's been listening to you all the time, my dear friend, hasn't she?" Helping the doctor out of his seat, Peterson was now asking for more precise details.

"She now knows everything including the fact that our colleague is looking for the second part of the medallion. These Blackdales have a global network. They are using modern technology to follow all our plans. We need to phone our colleague, Dr Robinson."

"Don't worry so much, my dear friend. Look, this elderly tourist has offered to take you to the town. Don't call the police. My associates and I should be left to complete the task we have been working on for many centuries."

Suffering from severe shock, and following his injection, Dr Silver lay back and rolled his eyes to the sky, muttering to himself.

***

The Legend of Cascard the Monk

In search of new lands and islands, Cascard the monk and ten of his peers gathered their possessions and the most secret prayers of the ancient pagans, and set off in a tiny boat from the island of Iona. Relying only on intuition, they drifted for several weeks, and as their supplies of food and water began to run critically low, their hopes of finding new land also dwindled.

Of all the monks, brown haired and dark blue eyed Cascard was the most strong-willed and optimistic and it was he who first caught sight of the land on which they would build a new life.

"Look, an island! An island!" he cried with crazy happiness. The island was special, with a huge black volcanic rock protruding from its centre, and was later named Black Rock.

It was located not far from the mainland, and in the early morning before high tide, one could see a sandy path which led from the island to the mainland. The monks feared the residents of the mainland. They preferred to domesticate the quiet island, in the belief that it was here that they could best continue their mission. The rituals and prayers that the monks performed, as well as the construction of their first altars, absorbed all of their time during the early months of their settlement.

One day, Cascard descended into a tunnel, thereby discovering the secret of the island, an underground route to the mainland. On one of his subsequent explorations of the tunnel, he was astonished to discover a natural source of precious stones and decided to gather a selection with which to embellish the altar.

In addition to developing his knowledge of the land, he was also keen to integrate with the local community and would regularly adopt the working clothes of the farmers to help with the harvest in return for a share of the crops.

It was during his time spent with the farmers that Cascard introduced them to the monks' old secret recipe for the "water of life", made and used for medicinal purposes but this was not well received by his own community.

"Why did you betray the secret of 'water of life'?" reprimanded the oldest monk, with furrowed brows.

"Holy Father, is it not our mission to assist ordinary people?" answered Cascard deftly.

"But these ignorant people are incapable of ever gleaning enough knowledge or skill to make it correctly and their attempts will dilute the true medicinal value of the original recipe which we monks have protected for centuries."

"That is just a matter of time. You yourself taught us that any business requires time, passion and dedication, did you not?" asked young Cascard.

These arguments left the old monk feeling powerless but he came up with a cunning plan.

One day, the worried old monk ordered Cascard to descend into the tunnel to collect precious gems, telling him they would be used for building another altar. Suspecting nothing, Cascard entered the tunnel and as soon as he was out of sight, the other monks blocked up the entrance with the intention of burying him alive.

Thus Cascard received his punishment.

Days passed. Cascard's loud and imploring requests for mercy could be heard from the depths of the tunnel. Eventually, ignored, emaciated and exhausted, he prepared to meet his death.

But suddenly, just as he lost all hope, his eyes were blinded by the bright light of the sky as the rocks were pulled from the mouth of the tunnel and a stranger, dressed in a helmet adorned with the horns of an animal, hauled his body outside.

The Vikings had arrived and seized the island and Cascard was horrified by the sight that awaited him: the decapitated bodies of all of the monks had been strewn along the shores.

Fearing a similar fate, Cascard did not hesitate to re-enter the caves under the orders of the chief, to gather a hoard of precious stones for the invaders who had already stripped the altar of those which Cascard had collected earlier.

For many days, the Vikings waited for him to return, but after a while, gave up, believing that either the underworld had claimed him or that huge waves had washed him away.

A few weeks later, something extraordinary happened: one of the Vikings awoke to hear their chief pleading for mercy and the next morning, found him slain by the entrance of the tunnel. Terrified that they too, would all be killed by the ghost of the monk, they fled the island.

According to ancient legend, the soul and spirit of Cascard the monk lives on to this day…

***

Having sat until evening imprisoned in the dungeon, watching the sunset through a small aperture, J.M. suddenly remembered the legend.

With a grin, she decided to conduct an experiment. Fashioning a monk's habit from an old grey blanket. It had been thrown to her by the Blackdale's clan chief earlier, with the fierce warning: "Keep yourself warm. You'll be here for some time and it gets really cold at night…"

Moving aside an old chair, she was able to hook up the garment so that it would be intermittently backlit by the flickering single bulb hanging from the ceiling in her cell.

She took off her shoes, and began to make strange sounds.

One of the guards, hearing the noise, quietly opened the door to see what was going on and catching sight of the "ghost" took fright and hysterical, began screaming for help from the Blackdales' clan chief.

At this point J.M, who had positioned herself behind the door, used all her strength to slam it against the guard, knocking him to the floor.

"Help! Monk Cascard has returned!" he cried, as he lay on his back with a broken nose and bleeding face.

J.M. immediately took the opportunity to race from the dungeon and up the stairs until she found herself in a long corridor on the ground floor of the ancient castle.

Meanwhile, arriving at the dungeon in response to the screams from the guard, the chief was furious to discover that JM had disappeared and that the cell was now only occupied by a scarecrow of sorts and an injured guard.

"Damn it! What are you playing at!" she yelled.

"A ghost, I saw a ghost, help me! It broke my nose!" the guard repeated these lines over and over, heedless of the enraged reprimands from the Blackdales chief.

"Where is the prisoner? Where is the silver lamp? Tell me!!" shouted the head of the Blackdales, shooting the guard in the leg in furious frustration.

Now the guard began to moan and cry, clutching his injured leg and ignoring the questioning.

"What is this? Have you completely lost your mind? What ghost? It's just a blanket; an old stinking blanket!" She waved his revolver in the guard's face and rushed up the stairs in pursuit of J.M.

Just as the chief was leaving, John Peterson and his friend Steven were lifting the iron hatch in the same small dungeon cell. They climbed through the basement area, where the old underground tunnel was located.

John Peterson helped his friend get out and saw the guard in the corridor. He was crawling on the ground with his wounded leg and broken nose and was still muttering about a ghost.

Seeing the feeing Blackdales chief, John Peterson lunged towards her and commanded:

"Hands up or I will shoot!" He pointed his gun at the Blackdales' chief's head, and she froze on the spot, still holding the old revolver in her hands.

Running up from behind, Steven grabbed the old blanket and flung it over the Blackdales' chief's head. The old woman started falling down the stairs, arms flailing and firing her old revolver erratically as she tumbled.

"My mother has told me so many times to respect the elderly, but I don't think this applies to an armed and evil old woman who would have no hesitation in shooting us!" joked Steven as he disarmed the chief.

"Well, what are you waiting for? Run off and save your Miss J.M.!" continued Steven winking at his friend John.

"We've been fighting to rid the world of these Blackdales vultures for so many centuries, but it is impossible to destroy evil completely."

Thanking his friend, Peterson ran up the stairs to catch J.M.

Everything then happened at once.

"Miss J.M.!" called Peterson. "Wait – don't open the door." He ran to hug the girl.

This unexpected turn of events threw J.M. into complete confusion, and she tearfully showered her rescuer with greedy kisses.

Peterson kept on apologising for the delay, repeating that the underground tunnel was much longer than they anticipated.

"Steven will call the police to arrest the Blackdales' chief and recover everything they have hidden in the dungeons. There's no point in us appearing in the press, until we have fully resolved your mystery, dear Miss J.M." Explaining the situation to his associates, John Peterson also recommended that they leave quietly and inconspicuously.

Chapter XI

"By the Water…"

"Right, so Steven stayed with the others to be interviewed by the police." Dr Silver was enjoying this conversation about the events which had followed his return to the city, and holding his wounded leg, he poured a fresh coffee for his friend Peterson.

Switching on the news, J.M exclaimed:

"Oh my God! Look, they're showing the head of the Blackdales vultures and that guard with a bandage on his nose. They've even found the works of Adam Smith!" All three were watching the morning news with great excitement, and laughing loudly. They were euphoric after the extraordinary adventures they had been through over the last twenty four hours.

They then turned their attention to the voice message from Dr Craig and the same old map that had been an unexpected find in the basement of the fisherman's house.

"Hold on, look here," exclaimed Dr Silver, turning the map towards J.M. and Peterson.

He pointed at the number 507 and typed something on his laptop. He had made an extraordinary discovery:

"I can't believe it: this is the height and width of the Alps!" said Dr Silver in great excitement.

"Wait a minute," interrupting the conversation, J.M. called Dr Craig Robinson.

"Hello, good morning, Dr Robinson. Could you please tell me more about the map which you found? Yes? Really?" J.M. continued to bat her long eyelashes in astonishment.

"Yes, yes. The same number is here on our old map. We found it in the old fisherman's house close to the old cave containing the labyrinth and of course, the most exciting thing of all, was finding the silver lamp recorded by Daria herself! Can you imagine? Assumptions about her arrival in Scotland with missionaries appear to have been proven by information contained in an old letter." JM was beaming with pride.

Dr Craig's valuable find had already been documented, with the assistance of the British Embassy, and he was now planning to wait for them in Denmark, to investigate the whole story further. They started to pack.

Dr. Craig had a very simple plan. He had discovered an old church in the small town of Tawlov in the Danish countryside in which there was an underground museum containing a large collection of very rare and unique antiques. Some of them dated back to the mid -sixteenth century and if the museum also held data concerning objects made by one particular master craftsman, it could offer them the vital clue they needed to unravel the whole mystery.

.... They were already packing to leave, and hurriedly typing on their laptops. They were both excited and hopeful about the possibility of making any small discovery that would help them find a conclusion to this story. The entire research process and all their hard work was at last making definite progress, and might soon bear fruit.

"The key word is 'Eschen', the name of a small settlement in the Alps. We have two leads: the number 507 and the word 'eshen' which translates as 'by the water'. The other clue is Liechtenstein!" The three of them shouted with joy.

"But, what is the significance of this small village?" Dr Silver puzzled, as he rubbed his tired eyes.

"Perhaps those numbers are the key, so let's start there. We will also need to learn more about the second part of the medallion that Craig found. If we are very lucky we will find the first part of the gold medallion, or something else made by the same master, in this underground museum. Then we could be really close to finding out what happened to the precious books brought and hidden by Daria," J.M. mused, excitedly.

"This is fantastic!" Limping on one leg, Dr Silver had already booked tickets on the internet for two: his friend John and J.M.

"The next little clue is the wonderful little country of Liechtenstein! What a pity I cannot come with you, but I'm entrusting you fully to my friend John Peterson, a real 'white knight'."

Winking, Dr Silver helped J.M. to pack up her papers.

"By the way, my dear friend, I would like to thank you for your parcel." Patting his friend on the shoulder, Dr Silver insisted on accompanying them to the airport, despite their entreaties.

***

The cabin was filled with the soft sound of jazz blues and having fastened her seatbelt, J.M suddenly felt utterly exhausted and happily turned her head to rest on John Peterson's shoulder. Drifting towards sleep, she smiled involuntarily as out of the blue, the image of the three people from the antiques shop appeared in her mind: the cheery grey-haired dealer and his two visitors. She suddenly felt much closer to recognizing them.

"…Hmm, wait a minute. Can there really be a parallel life?" she pondered. After all, just a moment ago, the image of the clerk Miller had appeared before her, or was it the old man whom the almond-eyed Nasipa had predicted would save Kara-Choro ?

"And the two visitors at the antiques shop: who were they? Hmm. Could they have been reincarnations of Tagay-bii and Tomchy? If so, that makes everything all right. They lived in another time, in another era, in another parallel world, and yet, they were still together…"

Closing her eyes, she continued to dreamily turn it all over again and again in her thoughts and now felt for certain, that they were close to unravelling the mysteries passed down through her family that had had such a profound impact on world history.

The end.

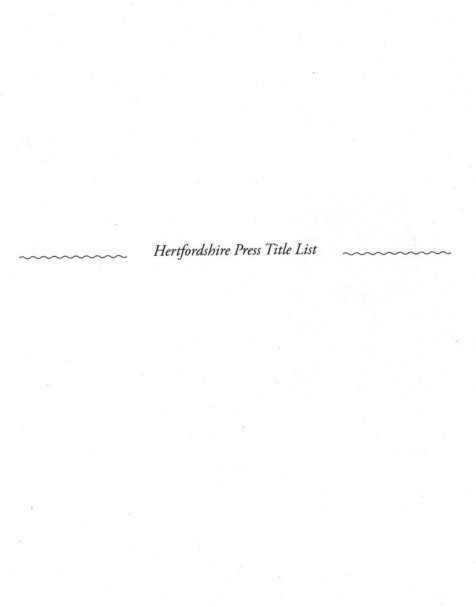

Hertfordshire Press Title List

WHEN THE EDELWEISS FLOWERS FLOURISH
by Begenas Sartov

The author frequently explored the tension between Soviet technological progress, the political and social climates and Kyrgyz traditions in his work, and When The Edelweiss Flowers Flourish depicts an uneasy relationship between two worlds.

Using the science fiction genre, the novel's main character is Melis – derived from Marx, Engels, Lenin and Stalin – who has his counter in Silem, an alien being sent to earth to remove Edelweiss plants to help save his own planet from a deadly virus.

The essence of the story was attributed by Begenas to a childhood experience when a village elder helped him recuperate from breaking his arm, using a herbal mixture of seven grasses. These grasses – Edelweiss, Ermen, Ak kadol, Shyraajyn, Oo koroshyn, Kokomirin and Shybak – are still found in the high Kyrgyz mountains today, and are still widely used for their medicinal properties.

RRP: £12.95
ISBN: 978-0955754951

FRIENDLY STEPPES: A SILK ROAD JOURNEY
by Nick Rowan

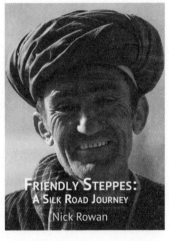

This is the chronicle of an extraordinary adventure that led Nick Rowan to some of the world's most incredible and hidden places. Intertwined with the magic of 2,000 years of Silk Road history, he recounts his experiences coupled with a remarkable realisation of just what an impact this trade route has had on our society as we know it today. Containing colourful stories, beautiful photography and vivid characters, and wrapped in the local myths and legends told by the people Nick met and who live along the route, this is both a travelogue and an education of a part of the world that has remained hidden for hundreds of years.

Friendly Steppes: A Silk Road Journey reveals just how rich the region was both culturally and economically and uncovers countless new friends as Nick travels from Venice through Eastern Europe, Iran, the ancient and modern Central Asia of places like Samarkand, Bishkek and Turkmenbashi, and on to China, along the Silk Roads of today.

RRP: £14.95
ISBN: 978-0-9557549-4-4

100 EXPERIENCES OF KYRGYZSTAN
Text by Ian Claytor

You would be forgiven for missing the tiny landlocked country of Kyrgyzstan on the map. Meshed into Central Asia's inter-locking web of former Soviet Union boundaries, this mountainous country still has more horses than cars. It never fails to surprise and delight all who visit. Proud of its nomadic traditions, dating back to the days of the Silk Road, be prepared for Kyrgyzstan's overwhelming welcome of hospitality, received, perhaps, in a shepherd's yurt out on the summer pastures. Drink bowls of freshly fermented mare's milk with newfound friends and let the country's traditions take you into their heart. Marvel at the country's icy glaciers, crystal clear lakes and dramatic gorges set beneath the pearly white Tien Shan mountains that shimmer, heaven-like, in the summer haze as the last of the winter snows caps their dominating peaks. Immerse yourself in Central Asia's jewel with its unique experiences and you will leave with a renewed zest for life and an unforgettable sense of just how man and nature can interact in harmony.

ISBN: 978-0-9574807-4-2
RRP: £14.95

THE GODS OF THE MIDDLE WORLD
by Galina Dolgaya

The Gods of the Middle World, the new novel by Galina Dolgaya, tells the story of Sima, a student of archaeology for whom the old lore and ways of the Central Asian steppe peoples are as vivid as the present. When she joints a group of archaeologists in southern Kazakhstan, asking all the time whether it is really possible to 'commune with the spirits', she soon discovers the answer first hand, setting in motion events in the spirit worlds that have been frozen for centuries. Meanwhile three millennia earlier, on the same spot, a young woman and her companion struggle to survive and amend wrongs that have caused the neighbouring tribe to avenge for them. The two narratives mirror one another, while Sima finds her destiny intertwined with the struggle between the forces of good and evil. Drawing richly on the historical and mythical backgrounds of the southern Kazakh steppe, the novel ultimately addresses the responsibilities of each generation for those that follow and the central importance of love and forgiveness.

Based in Tashkent and with a lifetime of first-hand knowledge of the region in which the story is set, Galina Dolgaya has published a number of novels and poems in Russian. The Gods of the Middle World won first prize at the 2012 Open Central Asia Literature Festival and is her first work to be available in English, published by Hertfordshire Press.

ISBN: 978-0957480797
RRP: £14.95

"THIRTEEN STEPS TOWARDS THE FATE OF ERIKA KLAUS"
by the National Writer of Kyrgyzstan, Kazat Akmatov

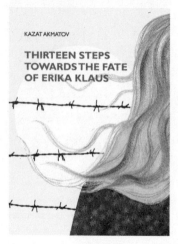

Is set in a remote outpost governed by a fascist regime, based on real events in a mountain village in Kyrgyzstan ten years ago. It narrates challenges faced by a young, naïve Norwegian woman who has volunteered to teach English. Immersed in the local community, her outlook is excitable and romantic until she experiences the brutal enforcement of the political situation on both her own life and the livelihood of those around her. Events become increasingly violent, made all the more shocking by Akmatov's sensitive descriptions of the magnificent landscape, the simple yet proud people and their traditional customs.

Born in 1941 in the Kyrgyz Republic under the Soviet Union, Akmatov has first -hand experience of extreme political reactions to his work which deemed anti-Russian and anti-communist, resulted in censorship. Determined to fight for basic human rights in oppressed countries, he was active in the establishment of the Democratic Movement of Kyrgyzstan and through his writing, continues to highlight problems faced by other central Asian countries.

RRP: £12.95
ISBN: 978-0955754951

MUNABIYA AND SHAHIDKA
by Kazat Akmatov, National Writer of Kyrgyzstan

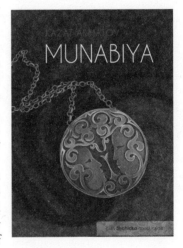

Recently translated into English Akmatov's two love stories are set in rural Kyrgyzstan, where the natural environment, local culture, traditions and political climate all play an integral part in the dramas which unfold.

Munabiya is a tale of a family's frustration, fury, sadness and eventual acceptance of a long term love affair between the widowed father and his mistress.

In contrast, Shahidka is a multi-stranded story which focuses on the ties which bind a series of individuals to the tragic and ill-fated union between a local Russian girl and her Chechen lover, within a multi-cultural community where violence, corruption and propaganda are part of everyday life.

RRP: £12.95
ISBN: 978-0-9574807-5-9